P9-DVV-531

Resourse

Level II

The Kid
Who Ran
for Principal

The Kid Who Ran for Principal

by Judy K. Morris

Published by The Trumpet Club
666 Fifth Avenue, New York, New York 10103

Copyright © 1989 by Judy K. Morris

ISBN: 0-440-84170-4

Reprinted by arrangement with J. B. Lippincott Junior Books,
imprint of Harper & Row, Publishers
Printed in the United States of America
January 1990

10 9 8 7 6 5 4 3
OPM

For Dora Downes and for Wilma Bonner,
In whose classrooms I learned how good school can be.

And in loving memory of my nephew
Nick
Who taught me the meaning of broken lockers, unrepaired.

Contents

The Kid
Who Ran
for Principal

1

A Good Little Girl

Once upon a time, though not so many years ago, not so far east of here and not so far west, there lived a good little girl named Bonnie Mann.

It was evening. Bonnie sat on the steps of her family's back porch watching the sky, for her father had mentioned that the moon would be full. The air was soft, with just a hint of action, as if a breeze were touching leaves somewhere down the alley.

Bonnie had made her last phone call of the day to her best friend, Jane; she had finished reading her last book of the summer. Now she had nothing to do but wait—wait for the moon to rise, wait for bedtime—wait for tomorrow, the first day of her last year at Daniel Webster Elementary School.

She touched her book, wishing she could go back deep inside the story. She looked at the few, sad flowers left among the weeds, then began to pick at the porch railing where the paint was flaking off. She thought of her friends, of homework tomorrow night, of school. She made a face at the man in the moon, as he peeped through the branches of the crab apple tree that grew beside the garage.

Down the alley, a dog lifted a long howl into the night. Bonnie felt goose pimples rising on her arms. When the dog's cry changed to a low growl, then to sudden, fierce snarls, she looked around uneasily and listened for running footsteps or a shout.

Instead, a strange silhouette slowly emerged from behind the garage. Bonnie saw first a long, tilted ladder, dark against the bright moonlight, then the short, slim man who was carrying it. He barely moved along the alley, for he was engrossed in the book he was reading, reading by the light of the moon.

The man stopped altogether and rested the ladder on the ground as he finished and then turned a page. Then, holding the book open under his arm and hooking his elbow around a rung of the ladder to steady it, he relit his cigar. As he bent over the cupped hands that held the lighted match, Bonnie recognized the straight hair hanging long from under the cap, the baggy coveralls, the slightly stooped posture. "Mr. Lipchik!"

The man finished working his cigar tip to a bright ember before he looked up, giving Bonnie time to wonder if she had made a mistake, time to wonder, even if this was Mr. Lipchik, why she had called. She had always thought Mr. Lipchik was a little strange, and tonight he seemed almost mysterious, coming as if by magic, just as she was thinking about school.

In all her years at Daniel Webster, she had spoken to Mr. Lipchik only when a teacher had asked her to find him and report a stuck window or a radiator that wasn't working. Bonnie would hunt for him along the empty halls, then outside front and back, and then, if she still hadn't found him, down in the little room in the basement where he sat and read.

From the first time she'd seen it, in second grade, his room had meant a lot to her. She loved knowing that one person, deep down under the school, had a place just the way he liked it, a place with a large, soft chair, a place to put his feet up, while everyone else, grown-ups and kids, sat in hard, straight chairs behind their desks. She liked thinking there was one person who could finish his chapter without being told it was time to stop.

Still, Bonnie had never said one word of her own to Mr. Lipchik, before tonight. Her calling to him, she realized much later, was the first unusual event in that whole extraordinary school year.

She held her breath, almost hoping he hadn't heard. She wondered what he talked about, when he talked.

"Evening," he said. His soft voice sounded as shy as she felt. He stared at her. "You from school?"

"Yes." She moved toward the alley fence.

"Is there a problem? Somebody call?"

"No. I just said hello."

"People have been calling me all day. The teachers were all at school, fussing at me, putting up their bulletin boards, cleaning out their cupboards. I found a few books." He pulled a leaf off the crab apple tree to mark his place and reached back over his shoulder to put his book into his lumpy knapsack. "I'll be glad when you all get there," he said. "They can go after you instead of me."

"I won't be. Glad."

"Don't like school?" He chuckled and rested a foot on the first rung of the old wooden ladder.

"I love school! But . . ." She wondered if she should say it.

"Whose class will you be in?"

"Mr. Locke's."

"Oh. Oh, well. Yes." Mr. Lipchik sent up a spout of cigar smoke. "Of course, he doesn't bother me much. It's the others."

Bonnie could imagine Miss Cherry and Mrs. Atkins fussing at Mr. Lipchik. She whispered, "Nothing good's going to happen all year."

"Oh, I don't know." He thought a minute. "Who'd you have last year?"

"Mrs. Tilley." Was it possible that Mr. Lipchik didn't know that Mrs. Tilley, fifth, came before Mr. Locke, sixth? "Nothing exactly happened last year, either, but I was class president, and Mrs. Tilley was wonderful."

"Mrs. Tilley has a smile!" Mr. Lipchik nodded. "Myself, I left school after fifth grade."

"Really!" Bonnie had heard of people doing that. "How . . . ?"

Mr. Lipchik puffed for a minute. "Now, you wouldn't have to go *that* far, but anyone can play hooky once in a while." He looked at her, hard.

Someone from a school encouraging her to play hooky! Mr. Lipchik really was strange.

"But I guess you wouldn't even do that," he said. "A good little girl like you."

"Can you tell?" Bonnie was appalled.

Mr. Lipchik nodded sympathetically.

Did it show, so she could never get away from it? Would everyone she ever met in her whole life know?

Bonnie had always been good. In first grade, she could still remember, she had watched Jerry and Jane and Nancy mix mud into water in a cup and tell a new kid it was chocolate milk. Bonnie couldn't bring herself to help her friends, but she hadn't warned the new kid, either, because that would have been bad, too, that would have been telling. She had just watched while the poor kid took a gulp of the disgusting stuff. She could still feel her shame.

"I don't try to be good," she told Mr. Lipchik. "It just happens." This very afternoon, downtown with Jane and Shawna and Nancy and Gillian, the others had run across a one-way street against a red light when there was absolutely no traffic coming. Bonnie had stood on the curb, waiting for the light to change, cringing as her friends teased her from the other side. An old lady, also waiting, had patted her shoulder and said, "Don't worry, dear. You're the good one. You're the smart one." When the light changed, Bonnie had rushed away from the old lady without saying a word.

"Tell me what it's like, being good," Mr. Lipchik asked.

"Don't you know at all?"

"Can't say I do. In my day, in my town, it was bad boys and good girls. That was pretty much expected. The line was clear, and I worked my side of the line." He grinned. "Being bad can be useful; it gives you a certain confidence. There's a flexibility to it."

"You're good now."

"I keep the school going, yes. But I do my ·work as I believe it ought to be done; I pretty much keep the freedom to be where I want to be and hear what I want to hear. Certain people have complained, but I pay no mind. The job gives me time to study. History is my field. Of course history doesn't teach me a whole lot about being good."

"Well, being good," Bonnie said. "My problem is, I get stuck in it. Everyone expects it. My parents and the teachers, the kids, they all trust me. My reports say I'm such a cooperative, responsible member of the class. It's nice and everything"—

Bonnie could hear her voice grow doubtful—"but it's like I don't do very much. Like that's all I am: good."

"I see the problem," Mr. Lipchik said. "But you have your whole life before you. History teaches: Things can be changed. You may do something they call bad and be a credit to yourself yet."

Bonnie made a question of her face, and Mr. Lipchik motioned in the direction of school. "Make some changes."

"At D-W? But everyone says it's a good little school," Bonnie said.

"Yes, well. That may be. Depends on what you mean by good." He looked at his cigar. "I expect something's going to happen over there. I really expect something's *got* to happen. The question is what, and how? Maybe you'll be the one to do it." He winked. "If you're not too good."

Bonnie had often wondered, in her eleven years, what it would be like not to always be so good.

"Here." Mr. Lipchik leaned his ladder against the garage, then set his large knapsack on the ground. He began lifting out books and piles of damaged construction paper and broken boxes that leaked pieces of puzzles and games.

"Here," he said again, and over the back fence he handed her a packet of mimeographed pages with a round coffee stain on its blue cover. "Don't know why I took this. Mr. Locke's wastebasket." He began restuffing the knapsack.

"Thank you!" Bonnie said. " 'Board of Education: Bylaws,' " she read out loud. "What's it for?"

"That might be some use to you," Mr. Lipchik muttered. He hoisted his knapsack onto his shoulders.

He doesn't answer straight, she thought, and he talks so mumbly around his cigar, it's like he doesn't care whether I hear or not. She asked, a little louder, "What are bylaws?"

"Rules, regulations, the laws they *go by*. Elections and all that. I'd better go." He picked up his ladder.

"Hey!" Bonnie said quickly, but when he turned, all she could think of to say was, "See you in the morning."

"I hope not. No offense, but I plan to get out of the way, again, once the children are back." He swung around, the ladder pointing his way down the alley. "Evening."

Bonnie watched him go, he and his ladder moving slowly in and out of moonlight and shadow, and heard him humming a tune she didn't quite recognize.

She flipped through the pages he had given her, thick with print. "Bylaws!" she muttered. Then, as she turned to go indoors, her eyes moved over the mess of her mother's garden, and she said more loudly, "Elections!"

It wasn't that Bonnie cared much about the garden, but the whole house was in the same state. The

Manns lived in a quiet, pleasant neighborhood of a large and noisy city. Their house was comfortable enough, but it was just a little dusty and just a little shabby, and there were always three or four things that needed fixing. Bonnie was proud of her parents, but she secretly wished their home was as well kept as their neighbors'.

Her mother's commitment to good government was a trial to Bonnie and her family in several ways: the garden, for instance. Almost every spring, Mrs. Mann planted many flowers; then, almost every summer, she got involved in an election and began to neglect them. By election day in the fall, the little backyard would be a mess of weeds. Mrs. Mann often said the only crop she could raise well was children, and that was because children could learn to take care of themselves. Whenever Bonnie heard this, she felt proud, and just a little lonely.

Bonnie found her mother now, working in the basement with other volunteers, telephoning voters about the primary election just a few weeks away. Mrs. Mann made a kiss sign and held up her finger for Bonnie to wait. Hanging up, she had just time to reach up and give Bonnie a hug and say, "Good night, dear. Sleep well. You're a good girl, and I know you'll have a wonderful year!" Then the phone rang.

Bonnie ran all the way up to the little attic study where her father was bent over his diagrams. Light from his desk lamp shone off his glasses and his partly bald head and his large and complicated watch. A fan ruffled the papers as he worked.

When Bonnie kissed him, Mr. Mann looked up and smiled. "First day of school tomorrow?" When Bonnie nodded, he stood and presented her with a dozen brand-new NASA pencils, which he had all ready, bound with a red elastic. Mr. Mann's company had a contract with the National Aeronautics and Space Administration to design experiments for the astronauts to take to the moon. Bonnie knew the other children envied her, for in the years just after the first moon landing of 1969 the whole country was excited by the space program. But her father's job took him away so much, and he had to work so hard, that the only thing Bonnie really liked about it was the NASA pencils. She never loaned her NASA pencils, even to Jane. Mr. Mann gave her a big hug. "Good night, Bon. Have a good year. Sixth grade! I'm very proud of you."

As she got into bed, Bonnie smiled, comparing what each of her parents had said with Mr. Lipchik's thought that she might do something bad. If only I can! she thought. Mr. Locke's class might be the exact place for me to start not being so good.

She arranged her pillow and her covers just right, then cuddled down and opened the bylaws. Before she had read two long paragraphs of long words about officers and purposes and procedures, she was extremely sleepy. Why should I read such dull stuff?

she asked herself. Why should I do homework on my last night of vacation?

But after she had closed the pages and dropped them on the floor, she didn't go to sleep for a very long time. The next day was, after all, the first day of school, and her first day with Mr. Locke.

2

A Good Little School

When Bonnie woke the next morning, she leaped from her bed, then stopped still. She poured her barrette collection out onto the bureau top. Which barrettes would Jane be wearing? In a flash she was off to rescue yesterday's socks from the bathroom clothes hamper. She put on the shirt she had already decided not to wear, took it off, and put on another.

When she noticed the bylaws on the floor, she kicked them under the bed. Her mind was on far more urgent matters: Which sneaker laces to wear? Would Mr. Locke let her and Jane and Nancy and Shawna and Gillian sit together?

Finally, she stood in front of the mirror, looking exactly right. She had on her old favorite plaid pants and a new bright-green shirt. Her long brown hair was pulled back exactly even on both sides, and her socks exactly matched her shirt. She stood as tall as she could, but it seemed she hadn't grown over the summer, not even half an inch.

Forget that! she told herself, and raced for the

stairs. Then she was struck by the thought: School! and walked slowly all the way down.

School! Mrs. Tilley would be there, to talk with at recess. But in her classroom, day after day, hour after hour, minute after long, slow minute, would be Mr. Locke.

Bonnie wished she could tell her parents about him. She could tell them, of course, but . . . she was sure they would pay little attention.

She found Schaffer just leaving. Schaffer Mann was big for his age; in third grade, he was almost as tall as his sixth-grade sister. With a short heavy stick in his hand, he looked extremely tough as he headed for the door.

Mr. Mann followed. "Wait up, Schafe! Let me tuck in your shirt."

"You must finish your juice," Mrs. Mann said, handing him the glass.

Schaffer tolerated the fuss his parents were making, until he noticed Bonnie noticing his smile. Then he scowled.

"What's the stick for?" Mr. Mann asked.

Schaffer coughed an important cough, and his scowl deepened. "Third grade does cavemen. Remember?" He was gone.

"Good-bye!" Mrs. Mann called. "Why was he in such a hurry?"

"He has Mrs. Atkins this year," Mr. Mann said. "Her good influence has begun already."

"Except he forgot his lunch." They both laughed.

Bonnie was sorry for Schaffer—having Mrs. Atkins—but she was even more sorry for herself. She sat down hard, making a thump to get her parents' attention, and finally said it: "School is going to be awful this year. Mr. Locke is so . . ."

"You can't expect to have a Mrs. Tilley every year, Bon," Mrs. Mann said, "even at a good little school like D-W."

"Mom!" But she couldn't seem to explain what the problem was. Once last year when he had had playground duty, Mr. Locke had changed the rules for lining up, and when Jerry hadn't understood he had mocked him so badly Jerry had cried. Mr. Locke never liked to explain, he just liked to tell people what to do. Then when they didn't understand, he acted as if they were stupid. Bonnie shivered, remembering. "I don't see how I can survive!"

"If a man can go to the moon and survive," Mr. Mann said, "you can survive one year with a teacher who is less than perfect. You and Schaffer always do fine, with the good teachers and with the mediocre ones. Grumbling about school is an old American tradition. Remember when we read *Tom Sawyer*?" Mr. Mann laughed as he got up and patted Bonnie's shoulder. "Give Mr. Locke a fair chance to fool you; he may turn out to be just fine."

"But . . ." Bonnie remembered something that might impress her father: "He's supposed to be not so good at math."

"I'm sure Miss Cherry wouldn't have him in her

school if he weren't an adequate teacher. If you have trouble with math, I'll be glad to help. Say hello to Jane-Shawna-Nancy-Gillian for me."

"Daddy!" Bonnie ate a very little bit of breakfast before she set off, with her notebook and her lunch and Schaffer's and a scared feeling in her middle that she knew would remain until she was safe among her friends in the school yard.

She walked slowly along the quiet streets, past the rows of houses with their wide front porches, enjoying the shade that the huge old trees provided against the late summer sun.

Two small boys came hurrying up beside her. They were adorable: red-haired and blue-eyed, with the kind of face grown-ups put in advertisements for baby food and bicycles and soup. However, the adorable faces were frowning.

The older boy, his new plastic briefcase thumping against his leg, was in Schaffer's class. Bonnie was sure he was already worrying about the homework papers waiting on Mrs. Atkins's desk.

The younger brother, she thought, was still another Grimmet. There always seemed to be four Grimmets at D-W. Last year, a Grimmet had graduated from sixth grade, and here came the replacement, scared about starting kindergarten.

The Grimmets often looked anxious and worried. They took school very, very seriously. Each found a way to be a goody-goody—and to be sneaky. The one in the class behind Bonnie—she would be the fifth-grade Grimmet this year—was as solemn and mean and treacherous as a kid could be. At least I'm not good like the Grimmets are good, Bonnie thought. At least I have fun.

The boys passed her, barely glancing up, answering her "Hi!" as carefully as soldiers giving a password for safety.

A moment later, a thin, very tall girl passed her, walking knees out, toes out, awkward as could be. Her head was bent over the book she was reading, so only her short blond curls showed, and Bonnie was free to stare. The girl was the right age for school and heading in the right direction, though she carried just a library book, an apple, and a spiral pad with a fancy four-color ballpoint pen clipped to it. Bonnie was sure she must be a sixth grader. Poor kid, she thought, being new and getting Mr. Locke who picked on people who didn't know how to do things.

Bonnie was ready to be friendly, but when the girl hurried past without looking up, she turned sharply, cutting through three alleys, and soon came out half a block ahead of the stranger. By then, Bonnie had forgotten her, for she could hear the sounds of school.

She stopped at the edge of the sidewalk and looked down toward the children skittering every which way across the blacktop, the playground, and the grassy field like water bugs over a pond. Bonnie located Jane and Gilly and Nancy and Shawna lean-

ing on a small fence, talking and watching Bobby
Roberts and the other big boys shoot baskets. She
gave a squeal, and her friends ran squealing to meet
her.

Jane took one of the new barrettes from her own
long brown hair and traded it for one of Bonnie's.

"Are you two still doing that?" Shawna asked.

"Nothing else to do, the whole year long," Jane
said.

"He's so boring," said Nancy.

"He's so mean!"

"I hate teachers who never even notice what's
fair," Gilly said.

"Maybe he's more fair with his own class," Bonnie
said.

"Oh, you're so good," Jane said. "You won't have
any trouble."

Bonnie was annoyed. "What good is good, you
ninny! I'll still be bored."

"Maybe he's so boring," Nancy said, "it's like an
anesthetic. After a while we won't notice the pain."

They jabbered about other matters—Gilly
pointed out that the two broken swings still weren't
fixed ("those poor little kids"; "that's so mean!"); Jane
pointed out that Lucy Ann Anson had started wearing eyeliner ("it doesn't help"; "at all!")—but the
bell brought Mr. Locke back to everyone's mind.

Jerry Windsor tried to joke about him when he
bumped into Bonnie in the crush going in. "How
bad can he be? Just tell me where he wants my name

and the date on the paper. Printing or cursive? Pen or pencil? Once you know that stuff, the rest is all the same."

Bonnie laughed, but she could tell that Jerry was also scared that Mr. Locke's class wasn't going to be the same at all. She asked Jane to try to save her a seat, then walked toward the third-grade room.

D-W was a small school, with just one teacher for each grade. The rectangular building had two floors, each with a long central hall, with wide stairs at each end. The kindergarten through third grades were on the first floor, fourth through sixth on the second. The classrooms were large and pleasant, their windows shaded by tall and leafy trees.

Bonnie passed Miss Cherry's thin figure in a dark brown suit, but she didn't bother to say hello. The principal seemed to look just over people's heads as she passed quietly through the halls, her lips pressed together. Miss Cherry rarely smiled—at most she nodded, as she nodded to Bonnie now, without really seeing who was there.

In the third-grade room, the walls were filled to the ceiling with the fresh, bright colors of new displays: charts, rules, lists, suggestions. Bonnie recognized the dancing numbers decorating the math corner, the upper- and lower- case alphabets parading over the chalkboards. She remembered the encouraging phrases mounted here and there: "Books We Enjoy:" "September Plans. We Will: . . ." "Let's Find Out:" "We Will be Good Citizens. We

Pledge: . . ." She recognized the Children of Other Lands tacked in a bright circle on one wall and the life cycle of the frog on another. She recognized, also, the guilty feeling inspired by all this neatly displayed information that seemed to say firmly, accusingly, as if with Mrs. Atkins's voice: "Pay attention! Learn this!"

The third graders were already seated, some already copying the neat writing on the board. Mrs. Atkins had her hand on the shoulder of the boy who was speaking to her, and her eye on two girls whispering in the back row. Mrs. Atkins's suit was as plain as Miss Cherry's, though her figure was plumper and the suit was a cheerful blue. Her short, curly gray hair, Bonnie noticed, was slightly blue as well.

"Yes, Bonnie?"

"May I . . . ?"

"*Good morning*, Bonnie."

"Good morning, Mrs. Atkins. May I give Schaffer his lunch?"

Mrs. Atkins chuckled. "He'll be an unhappy young man if you don't. Schaffer! Thank your good sister."

As Bonnie put the lunchbox on his desk, Schaffer looked up startled, as if he didn't recognize her. "Thanks," he whispered and bent over his paper. His caveman stick was nowhere in sight.

Upstairs in sixth grade, Mr. Locke hadn't come yet, and few of the kids were seated. There was no work to do and certainly no one wanted any. Gillian and Nancy were busy drawing fast pictures on the empty chalkboard.

Bonnie wandered here and there, talking with people she hadn't seen since spring. She wasn't surprised to see the tall, thin girl at a rear desk. She was writing in her spiral pad, snapping different colored tips into place on her fancy pen.

A dip in the noise level told Bonnie Mr. Locke had come. She found him beside her, his cool blue eyes looking swiftly about the room, as if he expected to find every single person doing something wrong.

"Good morning, Mr. Locke," Bonnie said.

"Good morning," Mr. Locke said, without looking at her. He raised his voice. "Excuse me! From now on, I'll expect you to be in your seats and ready to work at eight forty-five."

Bonnie went quickly to the seat Jane had saved. She was glad to find Nancy on her other side and Shawna and Gillian also within range if Bonnie wanted to whisper or scribble in their notebooks.

Mr. Locke walked to his desk and put down his coffee cup.

"I forgot about his shoes!" Jane muttered.

The crepe rubber soles of Mr. Locke's shoes squeaked against the linoleum floor for the next hour or so, as he walked back and forth, tediously getting the class organized. From time to time, work stopped as the loudspeaker crackled on, and Miss Cherry spoke, slowly, distinctly, correctly. The new girl, Bonnie noticed, seemed to be the only one prepared for such a boring morning; mostly, she read her book. Bonnie could recognize the cover: *My Side of the Mountain*.

The only interesting news all morning was for Nancy: Mr. Locke mentioned that he would coach the school spelling team. "Good!" she whispered, "Maybe I have a chance, finally, with my own teacher! . . ."

After recess, Mr. Locke introduced the study of electricity, and the class learned what kind of teacher he was.

He began by explaining the difference between parallel circuits and series circuits. On the board he drew two diagrams of how electricity moved through the wires, from the battery, to the switch, to three little light bulbs and back to the battery.

Bonnie had no trouble with Mr. Locke's clear diagrams. Her trouble came when he tried to explain.

"In a series circuit, when you shut off the flow of electricity, all the devices on the circuit will go off together. Each device on a parallel circuit that is being operated by the current can be shut off by a separate switch," Mr. Locke said.

"Do you use a switch on a series circuit, too?" Bonnie asked. "Is a switch a 'device' or is a 'device' a bulb?" Several people murmured, clearly as confused as she.

"Listen carefully," Mr. Locke said. "Each *device* in a parallel circuit can be shut off by a separate *switch*."

When Jerry asked him to explain again, Mr. Locke used almost the same phrases a third time. He spoke loudly and extra slowly, as if to make clear that Jerry and anyone else who didn't understand simply wasn't paying attention. Soon everyone was talking, some explaining, some complaining.

"Look!" said a voice. "Say the light bulbs are people on a picnic, and the electricity is a plate of chocolate chip cookies."

Every head in the room turned to the rear; every voice was still; everyone stared at the new girl.

"A series circuit is like when the people eat sitting on a fence, passing the cookies along; no one can get theirs till the person before gets theirs. One wire brings electricity through each light bulb to get to the next.

"A parallel circuit," she said, "is like when the people sit in a circle around the plate; everybody can grab for cookies at the same time. Each bulb has its own wire bringing electricity."

"Gail, this is science, not cooking class," Mr. Locke said scornfully. "You people should be getting ready for junior high! We're dealing with scientific facts here. We can't compare electricity to cookies. That's nonsense!"

What the new girl had said had been helpful, Bonnie thought, feeling sorry for her.

"Why *not* compare electricity to cookies?" Gail asked. "If it helps you understand."

Wow! Bonnie thought. *She* doesn't care about

being good, even on her first day! She didn't bother to listen as Mr. Locke, after a few more words for Gail, explained once more, his way.

Jerry waved his hand again.

"Study it, Jerry!" Mr. Locke said. "Study it on your own. I can't baby you along. We've spent enough time on this. Now, take out your math books."

Jane rolled her eyes at Bonnie.

That afternoon, language arts and American history were a little better. But then Mr. Locke handed out a series of worksheets, each of which Bonnie finished well before time was up, and the soft autumn sunlight coming through the window panes made her sleepy. She watched Jane put stickers over the old initials on her desk, then tape down a sign with her name and another with her schedule. Bonnie had forgotten how long a day at school could be.

The new girl, Gail, came running up beside Bonnie on the way home. "I thought you were in about fourth grade," she said, laughing. "That's why I walked by this morning."

Bonnie had no polite answer to that. The only reason someone might think she was in fourth grade was because she was short. Bonnie had never spent a lot of time thinking about how she looked: She didn't mind her plain, straight hair, and she didn't fret about her greenish-brownish, blah-colored eyes. But it seemed to her that a truly sensitive person would never even hint at the fact that she was four and three quarter inches shorter than the average girl her age. Still she managed to hold her tongue and not say anything rude.

Gail went on: "He was so dumb about the electricity! He almost had *me* mixed up about the circuits, and I had it just last year, in one of my schools."

"Do you move a lot?" Bonnie asked.

"My father has one of those jobs. I'm lucky to be here on the first day. But Mr. Locke! Are all your teachers so confused?"

Although she suddenly felt a sharp loyalty to Daniel Webster, once again Bonnie didn't argue. Instead, she asked Gail about herself.

Her full name was Gail Dewksbury, and her family had moved to the neighborhood just that week. Their house was right on Bonnie's way, as she found out when, in the middle of another of Bonnie's polite questions, Gail started up some steps.

"Hey!" Gail said. "I don't think I can last a year with Mr. Locke."

"Yeah," Bonnie said, "it's as if he likes to be mean."

"Well, he doesn't scare me. But . . . I don't think I can last." Before Bonnie could respond, Gail ran into her house.

So, Bonnie thought uncomfortably as she walked slowly on, there are *two* tough new people in our class this year: Mr. Locke and Gail.

3

One Big Bunch
of Nothing

Bonnie loved so many things about school and being with her friends that for several weeks she was mostly able to ignore the problems about Mr. Locke.

When she sighted Mrs. Tilley on playground duty for the first time, she shouted, "Mrs. Tilley! Charge!" and she and Jane and the others raced across the school yard and slammed against the fence.

"What do you think, Mrs. Tilley?" Jane asked. "Since we're the oldest grade now, don't we have to have a boy/girl party?"

"Ah!" Mrs. Tilley said. "It's boy/girl party time."

Bonnie would have been content to pass that milestone far in her future, but Jane had been eager for a boy/girl party ever since last year's sixth graders had come to school one Monday whispering loudly about the food consumed and the dances danced and the kisses kissed and the damage done to the house in question.

"Don't we have to?" Jane asked. "To get ready for junior high?"

"Oh, definitely," Mrs. Tilley said, taking off her sweater and stretching her arms in the autumn sunlight. "Absolutely. I'm just glad I had your class *last* year."

"I've got all the lists made," Jane said. "The food, the games, the records, the decorations, the people, the times, everything. But I don't know *where*. Gilly, how about yours?"

"They still say no."

"See, Mrs. Tilley?" Jane moaned. "Bonnie, can you ask again?"

"We can't. If he wins the primary"—and Bonnie suddenly hoped fervently that her mother's candidate would win—"she'll have election stuff all over the house till November."

"See!" Jane held out her places list. "There's nowhere on earth!"

"Jane! You've only asked me and Gilly and Nancy and Bonnie," Shawna said.

"Well, who do you want me to ask? A boy?"

"Sounds drastic, Jane," Mrs. Tilley said. "But if a man can go to the moon, I'll bet the sixth grade can manage to have a boy/girl party. Oh! Bonnie, I wish your father would call off those space shots!" Mrs. Tilley ran onto the playground to help a fallen child.

"10-9-8-7-6-5-4-3-2-1-0 Blast off!" was the favorite cry on the D-W playground in those years of the NASA moon landings, and pretending to be a spaceship was the favorite excuse for racing around. But too many spaceships going in too many directions could make the playground a dangerous place.

Now Mrs. Tilley gathered the would-be astronauts, appointed one child Mission Control, and declared that no astronaut could blast off without clearance.

Then the bell rang, and Mrs. Tilley turned to Jane. "Why don't you call it a 'class party'?" she suggested. "That sounds less threatening. You'd be more likely to find a place, and your dancing can be just as wild."

"Brilliant," Jane said to her friends as they headed for the door. "The woman is purely brilliant. She has all the great ideas."

In the classroom, Mr. Locke wasn't back yet from working with the spelling team. He and Nancy and Lucy Ann and the others who were trying out were often late from recess. Bonnie took out her math book and looked at the four homework problems that she still did not understand.

Bonnie shared with most of the class several complaints about Mr. Locke. Every day at recess, it seemed, someone groaned about how boring he was, and Gail mocked his confusing explanations. He got mad at Jerry often, picking on him until one day Jane couldn't stand it anymore and tried to come to Jerry's rescue. Mr. Locke shouted at her to stay out of it, and everyone sat fuming quietly in their seats.

But the worst thing about Mr. Locke, for Bonnie,

was a private problem. Math had always been her weakest subject, and Mr. Locke, over and over, explained the work poorly. Although her father helped her—when she asked, when he wasn't away—in many math classes, for long, almost unbearable periods, Bonnie just didn't understand.

At first, she had raised her hand when she needed help, and Mr. Locke had explained, exactly as he had explained before, exactly as the book explained, leaving her confusion exactly the same. But after a few questions, Mr. Locke's voice grew cool and hard, and Bonnie felt the class getting restless. She imagined "Dumb!" echoing in the minds of Bobby and Nancy and Gail and Walter and the other smart kids. Then she would nod silently and question no more. By the end of the second week, her confusion and her shame were so strong, she no longer asked at all.

Then, this day, there was a really bad math class.

Mr. Locke rushed in, a scowl on his face, and started math, as usual, by reviewing the times tables. He scribbled multiplication problems here and there on the board, with the class calling out the answers.

"Five times eight!" Mr. Locke shouted.

"Forty!" the class shouted back, and Mr. Locke slashed forty onto the board.

"Seven times four!" he shouted.

"Twenty-eight!" the class shouted back.

Anyone who didn't know seven times four by now must be asleep, Bonnie thought. Mr. Locke's brain seemed stuck on that one. He used it every single day. Nevertheless, she copied it down. Copying wasn't required, but she was determined to get better in math.

"Seven times nine!"

"Sixty-three!"

Bonnie noticed Mr. Locke's eyes begin to glaze over. Jerry had said the teacher was a walking zombie during the math shouts: "He goes on automatic pilot. Catching a nap while we work."

"Eight times zero!" Mr. Locke shouted.

There was a slight pause. Several voices said, "Zero," and one loud voice said, "Eight."

Mr. Locke drew eight on the board. "Six times six!"

"Thirty-six!" the class shouted, and Bonnie shouted loudest of all. That was her favorite, so neat, with all those sixes; it was the one she never got wrong.

Bobby Roberts had his hand up. Walter Byrnes had his hand up. Gail Dewksbury had her hand up.

"No hands. Just shout it out. You should know the rules by now," Mr. Locke said. "Seven times eight!"

The class shouted, "Fifty-six!"

But Gail was shouting, "Eight times zero equals zero!" which took longer, so her ". . . equals zero!" hung alone and strong in the air.

"Seven times eight is zero?" Mr. Locke's eyes opened a little wider.

"He's mad now. Gail's spoiling his little nap," Nancy whispered to Bonnie and Jane.

The teacher gave a bark of a laugh. "Wake up, Gail! Fifty-six."

"No!" Gail said, loudly. "Eight times zero is zero."

"Yes," said Walter.

"I wish Gail wouldn't do that," Bonnie whispered back. "He's going to jump all over her."

As Mr. Locke walked over to his desk, shoes squeaking, the class was silent, waiting for a storm. But he sipped his coffee and found the equation among the chaos of figures on the board. "Here it is. Eight times zero is eight," he read, in a cold, firm voice. He tapped with his chalk. "Pay attention, Gail. Seven times seven!"

Only a few voices answered, "Forty-nine." Most of the children depended on the confident voices of Walter and Bobby and Gail in the math shouts, but Walter and Bobby and Gail seemed to be more interested, at this moment, in eight times zero.

"That answer should be zero, Mr. Locke," Bobby said.

"Bobby, stop banging that desk!" Mr. Locke said. The desk was too small for Bobby Roberts's large frame. Several times a day, it got stuck up off the floor, resting on his knees, when he tipped his chair back, then thumped against the floor as he came forward again.

"But eight zeros . . ." Bobby said.

"Bobby, Gail! Use your eyes." Mr. Locke under-lined the troublesome equation, then circled it. "Come on, you people. Think!" He looked around the class. "Bonnie?"

Bonnie sat up, uneasy. What did he want?

"Eight times zero?" he asked.

Bonnie shook her head slightly. She just didn't know which answer was right. It seemed simple. It must be simple, but with Mr. Locke staring at her, and the whole class waiting, she was so panicked she couldn't get her brain to concentrate so she could figure it out.

Tap, tap, tap, went Mr. Locke's chalk against the board. He nodded at her, his fierce eyes holding hers, making her look back only at him, making her believe his answer must be right.

She knew what he wanted. She whispered, "Eight."

Mr. Locke nodded, releasing her eyes, but there was a hoot of laughter from the back of the room. Bonnie looked down at her desk.

"No!" Gail said again.

Nancy leaned close and whispered, "He's wrong! Why can't he just believe he made a mistake?"

Bonnie nodded, keeping her head down so her hair fell forward and Nancy couldn't see her eyes full of tears. Mr. Locke had made a mistake and didn't even know it, and he had made her make that mistake, too, and everybody saw. He had called on her because he could depend on her. Good little Bonnie would never say a teacher was wrong.

Mr. Locke was frowning at the equation.

"Eight times *one* is eight," Walter said. "Eight times *zero* is zero."

Mr. Locke didn't seem to be listening.

"Eight zeros," Bobby said. "Okay, add zero eight times, you get zero."

"Eight nothings is still nothing," Gail said. "All you get is one big bunch of nothing."

The class laughed uncomfortably.

Mr. Locke shook his head suddenly, still looking at the board, and Bonnie heard Nancy whisper to Jane behind her back, "I think he finally noticed."

Mr. Locke stepped briskly in front of the chalkboard and began erasing all the work into smears of chalk.

"All right," he said. "All right! Enough of that. You knew what I meant. Everyone knows multiplying anything by zero equals zero. I'm tired of a few of you taking advantage of every opportunity to disrupt the class. If any of you are still in doubt about the correct answer"—he looked over the class and his eyes rested on Bonnie—"I suggest you consult your books. Bonnie, you'd better review some fourth- or fifth-grade books. This is hardly sixth-grade material. Now. Take out clean paper for a quiz on last night's homework."

Bonnie stared at the list of equations she had copied from the board. "Seven times nine equals sixty-three," she had written. "Eight times zero equals eight," she had written. "Six times six equals thirty-six." The wrong answer between two right ones, and she hadn't known it. She looked to the board, but all that was left was a hodgepodge of little lines.

She had never felt so helpless, and so ashamed. If it hadn't been for Bobby and Gail and Walter, Bonnie would have believed eight times zero equals eight. Perhaps she would have believed it for the rest of her life.

Bonnie's humiliation stayed with her, and she left school quickly that afternoon. She was not happy to hear the sound of Gail's awkward steps running up behind. She snuffed and wiped and coughed and fixed things up as best she could before Gail caught up.

"Hey, what's with Locke and basic mathematics?"

Bonnie laughed and hoped her eyes weren't red. "I hate math."

"You hate it because of him. It's horrible when he explains it so people can't understand. Bonnie, you have to stand up to that guy when he's wrong."

"It was my fault. I didn't know he was wrong. I didn't understand until you all explained it. I just really didn't understand."

"It's *not* your fault! It's him. He knows math, he just doesn't bother to stay awake and teach it so people will get it. You have a right to have it explained. That's what school's for."

That made sense to Bonnie. A teacher should explain. Mr. Locke's way wasn't right, she thought. A teacher shouldn't be like that.

"He was using you!" Gail's voice was still angry. "He knew you'd say what he wanted you to. He's such a jerk, and he wastes so much time on stupid stuff, and I *have* to learn math, if I'm going to be a vet!"

"You are?" Bonnie envied a kid who knew her future.

"Yes," Gail snapped, "if Locke ever . . ."

They were at Gail's house. A woman in blue jeans and a pretty blouse was in the side yard, weeding and digging with a garden fork.

Gail introduced her mother. With a warm smile, Mrs. Dewksbury invited Bonnie in for a soda. But Bonnie wanted just to be alone in her own home. "I have to go, Mrs. Dewksbury, thank you."

That's really funny, she thought. Gail Dewksbury has a mother more regular than mine!

Fixing her after-school snack was the most peaceful, private moment of Bonnie's day. This afternoon, the job took persistence and creativity since in the heat of the election, Mrs. Mann rarely had time to go to the store.

Bonnie slowly inspected the leftovers, rummaged among the frosty hunks in the freezer, and checked every cupboard. By the time she brought a plate with three reheated barbecued chicken wings and some cottage cheese sprinkled with cinnamon into the dining room and thumped into a chair, she was feeling better.

"Did you find something? Oh, that looks good." Mrs. Mann looked up over her glasses, which continued to point down toward the index cards she was alphabetizing. "So, Hon, what did you learn today?"

Her mother always asked that, never a simple: "How was school?" Usually, Bonnie took the question for fun and tried to decide which was the single most important thing she had learned. Today, she said immediately, "Eight times zero is zero."

Mrs. Mann made a face. "I would have thought that was rather obvious. A thousand nothings is still nothing. Hey! We could use that. We need a good slogan." She made a note on one of the cards. "That man has been on the city council eight years and boasts about his experience, but eight nothings is still nothing."

"Gail said the same thing! Exactly."

Mrs. Mann laughed. "They say when people who don't know each other begin to get the same idea, the idea is ripe. Maybe my candidate has a chance of throwing the rascal out!"

"Gail said all you get is one big bunch of nothing."

Her mother laughed again and put that on her card as well.

"She meant Mr. Locke. He got that problem wrong," Bonnie said carefully, watching her mother's face. "He didn't know it, and the kids had to tell him."

Mrs. Mann looked up, eyes and glasses. She pushed her hair back from her face. But all she said, after a minute, was, "Well, I guess anyone can make a mistake. I'm glad you all were able to set him straight. Keep asking questions, Bonnie. I'm really proud of you."

Why? Bonnie thought. I didn't do anything. I was just good, and that turned out to be the dumbest thing of all.

4

Getting the Situation Straight

"Look!" Gail said one morning on the way to school. She pulled up her sleeve to show an ugly, swollen sore from a vaccination. "Isn't it great? I'm going to let it fester as long as I can. If anyone tries to mug me, I'll just flash my fester at him."

That was Gail, Bonnie thought. Cool enough not to be disgusted by the disgusting sore, smart enough to plan in case she got mugged, and bold enough to flash her fester at a crook. She told Jane the story at recess.

"How did Gail get like that, anyway?" Jane grumbled. "So smart about how to do everything?"

"I don't know. Maybe starting in new schools so much . . . ? Anyway, I bet you wouldn't care if she was helping you get the party!"

"Is she your friend?" Jane asked.

"No," Bonnie said. "Not exactly. It gives me shivers when she talks back to Mr. Locke, but . . . She's rude, but Jane, she's usually right. Anyway, she's interesting to walk with."

But going home one bright, windy afternoon, when Bonnie noticed Gail up ahead, she took care to walk slowly. She needed to be alone, so she could concentrate every bit of her attention on her favorite fall ritual: cracking acorns.

Huge willow oaks lined the streets on Bonnie's route between home and school. With their small, slim leaves, the trees didn't seem like oaks until the fall, when they dropped thousands of tiny acorns.

Bonnie accepted the acorns as a personal gift. Since kindergarten, she had loved the days when she could walk the entire way stepping on one acorn after another. She liked to feel the little acorn give under her shoe, to listen for the crack as it split, to count how many steps in a row she could take popping acorns. She walked slowly, her eyes scouting the sidewalk ahead.

Today, as she watched her left foot take her one hundred and twenty-first consecutive step onto an acorn, she noticed a piece of three-hole notebook paper lying directly in her path. On it she saw the word "Bonnie."

She looked up, as startled as if somene had shouted her name. There was no one to be see, no movement but willow oak leaves responding to the wind.

Bonnie picked up the page. The title was "6th Grade," but there was no subject name, teacher's name, student's name, and date in the upper right-hand corner, as Mr. Locke required. The "Bonnie"

headed a list, circled in red, with four other names :
Jane, Gillian, Nancy, and Shawna.

Bonnie smiled. How many times she had written
those five names herself, on birthday party lists, in
Valentine hearts, slumber party lists, club lists, or
just doodling around her notebook pages. Once Jane
had hidden the names over and over in a word-search
game.

The page had four other groups of names. "Lucy
Ann" headed the names of the girls who hung around
with Lucy Ann Anson and wore their sweaters the
way Lucy Ann wore hers, the girls who held their
long and shiny hair back with headbands, instead
of barrettes—a small difference, but all the difference, to Bonnie. "The ones who think they're so
great," she muttered.

"Bobby" headed the third group, the four big boys
who dominated the blacktop. Bobby Roberts was
such a good athlete and so friendly, he was the natural leader of the class. Although he was a little
awkward and a little overweight, although he didn't
wash his dark hair or have it cut as often as he might,
Bonnie didn't mind. The others were rougher, teasing boys—none as nice as Bobby.

The largest group had "Jerry?" at the top. Here
were the names of most of the remaining boys of
the class, not a group so much as a pack. Along with
a few fifth graders, they had chosen teams at the
first day's first recess and hadn't missed a moment
on the basketball court since.

Jerry was the liveliest and funniest of the smaller boys. He was the shortest boy in the class, as Bonnie was the shortest girl, and they had become good friends over years of being stuck at the front or the end of various lines.

At the bottom of the page, a few other people were listed: two quiet girls who walked together and sat together but never seemed to do much else; Michael Burney, who whined, and sharpened his pencil at the beginning of every period, and had no friends; and a few others.

This paper described her class exactly, and Bonnie guessed immediately where it had come from: Mrs. Tilley had made it for Mr. Locke, to help him understand the class he would be teaching. Then Mr. Locke, the ninny, had lost it.

Bonnie couldn't wait to show the list to Jane; then she decided she wouldn't. Jane might think *she* should have been listed as the leader of their group, and maybe that was right. Certainly, Jane phoned the most and made the most lists and plans. Jane had been the one who had pointed out, at a terrific pajama party in fourth grade, that the five of them *were* a group. Bonnie remembered, and smiled, and raised her eyes, and looked right into the face of Gail Dewksbury.

"Did I get it right?" Gail asked.

It took Bonnie a moment to understand. When she did, she was shaken, and confused, and not a little angry.

Who was this stranger, anyway—this new kid who thought she was so smart, who thought she could mark them all down, as if she were a god and the others were just little names at the end of her fancy pen? Gail had everyone lined up so neatly, as if she knew everything about them. It wasn't her business, anyway, Bonnie thought, who was friends with who.

She looked down at the page. Separating us onto little islands with her red ink! she thought. Jerry and I are friends, and where is *that* on Gail's chart?

What did Gail want? As Gail continued to stare at her, Bonnie shuddered with the feeling that something dangerous was going on. Clearly Gail Dewksbury had some plan for the sixth grade.

"Do you think it's some kind of a game?" she asked as coldly as she could. "You didn't put yourself in there. What are you doing it for, anyway? To see who could be your friend?"

"No, I'm not usually in any group. I make a chart whenever I get to a new school. Did I get it right?"

Bonnie couldn't lie. "Yeah."

"What about Jerry?"

"Those guys don't really have a leader; they just run around."

"I like to put someone. But isn't Jerry kind of stupid?"

"No!" Bonnie said. "Well, in class sometimes, but Jerry's great. He's not stupid at all. Put Jerry. But put Jane for us."

"That's what I thought, at first," Gail said. "But I'll leave you on."

"Mostly we just sleep over," Bonnie said, "and stuff." She wished she would stop talking, she wished she would just crumple up that paper and throw it in Gail's face and walk away. She wished just once in her life she could do something like that.

"What about those kids?" Gail pointed to the names at the bottom.

Bonnie felt as trapped as when Mr. Locke pulled her onto his side about eight times zero, pulled her with his eyes. "That's okay," she whispered.

"Okay," Gail said. "Thanks a lot." She put her hand on the paper.

Bonnie did not let go. She had found the list. Finders keepers.

Neither girl moved.

The third-grade and second-grade Grimmets raced past then, one after the other, yelling and scattering acorns.

"What's with them?" Gail asked. "There's one of them everywhere I step, like cockroaches."

A snort of recognition burst from Bonnie before she could stifle it. "They're Grimmets. There's Grimmets all over school. We're lucky we don't have one."

Gail nodded, then pulled gently on the list. "This is my only up-to-date copy. I'll make you one if you want."

Bonnie pushed the paper at Gail and moved away. "I know my own class!"

Gail was making green checkmarks on the page. Trying very hard, Bonnie managed not to say goodbye. She was determined to walk on alone. But after only a few steps, unable to stop herself, she turned and asked, again, "What is it, a game?"

Gail walked quickly up beside her. "I like to get the situation straight."

"Huh?"

"In case." Gail shrugged. "I just like to know how things are, just in case I need . . ." She said no more but continued to walk with Bonnie until they got to her house. There she called " 'Bye!" and ran up her steps as if nothing had happened between them.

All the way home, Bonnie stomped on every acorn in her path to a new rhythm: "Gail! Dewks! Bury! Gail! Dewks! Bury!"

For her snack, she made a great sandwich of leftover meat loaf, ketchup, chopped onions, and dill pickle slices. She poured a glass of apple juice and walked around the house as she ate.

In the dining room, she noticed that the city council primary campaign had moved into the final stage: When the basement got too crowded, Mrs. Mann brought the overflow election materials upstairs. At this point, only the sideboard was stacked with papers, but Bonnie knew that in a few days one end of the dining table would be covered. By election week, the family would be eating in the kitchen.

Bonnie looked over the familiar, boring piles: leaflets with the candidate's biography and positions on important issues; bags of bumper stickers and campaign buttons; stacks of posters, lists, and cards. The pattern of one list of names seemed familiar. With a start, Bonnie remembered where she had just seen a similar page, and she was bothered and angry all over again.

If Gail was figuring out the class so she could run for president, she thought, Gail could forget it. Bobby was due. He had been president in second grade and fourth, and he surely would be elected again this year. In the in-between years, Jerry, Lucy Ann, and Bonnie had been class president. Funny, Bonnie thought, that was just like Gail's chart.

5

The Truth about
Mr. Locke

Walking toward school a few days later, Schaffer
pulled the hood of his yellow sweatshirt down over
his face. "What I hate," he grumbled, "is I have to
waste so much time being polite to kids."

"Do the other kids have to be polite to you?"
Bonnie asked.

"Of course!" He yanked the hood back and
grinned. "Yesterday the Grimmet had to be polite
to me, also Jason, also Brandy Tibbets."

"How are the cavemen?"

"We're doing diet now. Hunting is fun, but the
four basic food groups are kind of stupid, for cavemen. Mrs. Atkins loves to sneak in that stuff." The
sweatshirt was back over his head. "And I hate doing
sheets. You sit down, you do your sheet from your
color card, you go hand it in, you get another card,
you sit down and do another sheet. Fridays are good.
Fridays she brings us cookies and reads stories."
Then he added, so softly Bonnie barely heard,
"There's so many *minutes* in third grade."

"Well, Schafe . . ." Bonnie started, but there wasn't really anything comforting to say, even if her parents did think Mrs. Atkins was such a great teacher. Soon Schaffer ran ahead to meet his friends.

On the playground, Jane reported indignantly that Mr. Locke wouldn't let the sixth grade have parties in his room once a month after school. Maybe, he had said. Once every other month? Maybe, he had said. Once? Maybe. "If he only would," Jane moaned, "it would solve my whole problem!"

"Jane!" Bonnie said. "Mr. *Locke* is the problem."

When the bell rang, Bonnie and her friends walked toward their classroom as slowly as they could while still technically being in motion.

When they got to the room, Bonnie wished they had run. Mr. Locke was absent, and Mrs. Tilley, for some reason, was taking over sixth grade for the day. She welcomed them all with a smile.

She started by giving the class a review of fractions, working in a businesslike way from addition of fractions through division of fractions. Bonnie whispered to Nancy: "Mrs. Tilley goes after the lowest common denominator like Jane goes after the boy/girl party!"

Mrs. Tilley finished off with a test, and soon the room was full of the small sounds of earnest concentration: the jiggling of a desk on a nervous leg; a pencil tapping, falling, rolling; feet moving on and off chair rungs; the brushing away of eraser crumbs.

Bonnie got an eighty, the best she had done in math all year.

When she looked up after the test, Mr. Lipchik was standing inside the classroom door. He was just standing, without a mop or a wastebasket, twisting his leather cap in his hands. His sandy hair showed gray at the sides, and his cigar, halfway smoked but out for the moment, rested behind his left ear. He wore green coveralls which were a little too short for him, showing his white socks. Bonnie was seeing him for the first time, she realized, since school started. He certainly knows how to keep out of the way, she thought.

Her mind went back to the interesting conversation she had had with Mr. Lipchik the night before school began. Something had to happen at school, he said, though he hadn't suggested what. Bonnie hoped the something would happen to Mr. Locke! But Mr. Lipchik has no power to change things, and neither, she thought, have I.

Mrs. Tilley explained that since she knew little about electricity, she had asked Mr. Lipchik to talk about the school's wiring system.

As soon as he started to talk and needed both hands to gesture with, Mr. Lipchik put his cap back on his head and seemed to lose his shyness. As the class piled on the questions, he told stories of famous short circuits, blackouts, electrical fires—plumbing disasters, too—at D-W and other buildings where he had worked. When he got his diagram mixed up, he asked Walter Byrnes to help; together they worked out sketches of the parallel circuits for the classroom lights. Walter asked if there were any series circuits in the school.

"You know that little supply room? Some jackass wired that one in series." Mr. Lipchik shook his head. "I have to take a flashlight to change a bulb in there."

"Sounds like an ideal field trip," Mrs. Tilley said. "No permission slips, no bus tokens, no buddy system, no lunches to lose, just there and back in ten minutes. Let's go!"

A few minutes later, twenty-four people crowded into the supply room, and Mr. Lipchik closed the door. He climbed on a table and put his hand on a bulb. "Ready?" He unscrewed the bulb, breaking the circuit. Instantly, all three lights went out. The class cheered.

Jane's voice came through the dark: "Chocolate chip cookies, all gone!" Oh, Bonnie thought, it feels so good to laugh. She and the others cheered again when Mr. Lipchik waved good-bye.

In the afternoon, Mrs. Tilley told the class she couldn't help them with the Alien and Sedition Acts nearly as well as Mr. Locke could. "I'll just leave that for him. So I thought we'd combine language arts and history. We'll read the Declaration of Independence. The Dec . . ."

She was interrupted by a low groan.

"Mrs. Tilley, we already did the Declaration," Lucy Ann said.

"Yes," Mrs. Tilley said. "But this is the basic document. There's always more you can learn."

She handed out copies, and the class reviewed them, dictionaries open, making sure the words were clear. Then Mrs. Tilley asked for a summary of the meaning.

"They're telling the whole world why they have to fight King George," Shawna said. "Also to get the other Americans to fight?"

Mrs. Tilley nodded. "Putting into words exactly what was upsetting people. Rallying the troops."

"Mrs. Tilley," Bonnie asked, "were the revolutionaries the good guys already? Then?"

Several big boys laughed. Bonnie had asked Mr. Locke the same question. "Of course, Bonnie!" he had said. "These are our heroes! Haven't you been to a Fourth of July parade?"

With Mrs. Tilley, Bonnie wasn't afraid of sounding dumb. "How could people *tell* the revolutionaries were going to be the good guys?"

"They didn't look like such big heroes at Valley Forge," Lucy Ann said, snickering. "They looked like bums, with holes in their shoes."

"Are all rebels bold and noble heroes?" Mrs. Tilley asked. "Or are they villains, tearing their country apart? Bonnie? Anybody?"

"It depends who wins."

The class laughed, but Mrs. Tilley said sharply, "No! No, Gail, be careful. Winning has nothing to do with good. Sometimes the good guys don't win, Bonnie."

"Yeah, Bonnie!" Gruff laughter came from the back. "So you might as well stop trying so hard."

"Shut up, Walter!" Nancy said.

"A revolutionary must decide for himself what's right," Mrs. Tilley said. "The American rebels weren't good guys because they won. They were good because they decided—each citizen—that the great ideals in the Declaration were so important they would live their lives by them, and fight, and even die for them."

"And then they did win!" Bonnie said.

"But they didn't *know* they would win. Just as they didn't know how history would judge them. You can only be sure that what you do is right. Then, be prepared to act and willing to do your best. Ben Franklin said it: 'Readiness is all.' "

After a moment's silence, Mrs. Tilley went on, "Challenging authority is hard. I don't know where all that lonely courage comes from."

She looked around the room. "Now! Let's feel the power of Thomas Jefferson's words! Stand up and read out!"

Gilly started: "When in the Course of human Events, it becomes necessary for one People to dissolve the Political Bands which have connected them with another . . ."

Gail's strong voice spoke the famous line: "We hold these Truths to be self-evident, that all Men are created equal, that they are endowed by their Creator with certain unalienable Rights, that among these are Life, Liberty, and the Pursuit of Happiness."

"Let's hear it for happiness!" Jerry shouted, and the class cheered. Bonnie grinned to see Jerry so happy after all his hard times with Mr. Locke.

So it went until Michael Burney slowly, carefully, read the last line: "And for the support of this Declaration . . . we mutually pledge to each other our Lives, our Fortunes, and our sacred Honor."

"Wow!" Walter said. " 'Our sacred Honor.' "

"Down with King George!" Gail yelled, and some kids banged their desks and hollered.

Bonnie looked around. Jane lay back, her feet stretched out; Bobby and Gillian had their eyes closed. Still, Bonnie was sure that for everybody, this had been the best day of sixth grade.

After school, Bonnie dawdled long enough to be the last one in the room. She went up to the teacher's desk. "That was great, reading out the Declaration."

Mrs. Tilley nodded. "Well, it got a bit rowdy, but I guess no one can complain about the noise if you're teaching the Declaration." She picked up a copy. "Franklin and Jefferson said almost everything worth saying about politics and human nature. It's up to the rest of us to remember and keep the faith."

"Math was good, too," Bonnie said.

"Do you like messing around with fractions?" Mrs. Tilley grinned. "I love the way they come out, so neatly."

Bonnie swallowed hard. "Mrs. Tilley, I'm having a hard time in math this year. I don't think Mr. Locke teaches math very well, explaining and everything."

Mrs. Tilley looked up at her and looked away.

Was Mrs. Tilley annoyed at a kid telling on another teacher? "Mrs. Tilley, he made a bad mistake!"

Mrs. Tilley laughed her bright laugh. "Oh, we all make mistakes. Please remember, teachers are human. And I believe he's awfully good at history. Did you point the mistake out to him?" Her eyes twinkled.

Maybe she's thinking how Mr. Locke must have looked when the kids told him he was wrong, Bonnie thought. But that had not been fun, that class. That class had been horrible.

"Some kids did. But I got confused. Even when he doesn't make mistakes, it's hard to understand what he means." Bonnie's throat felt tight, as if it was difficult to push out these words. "If we ask too many questions, he gets mad. It's like he just wants to get through, and he doesn't really care if we learn it."

Mrs. Tilley nodded slightly. "I see your problem."

"Jane has a list on him, all the bad things." Bonnie

felt better bringing in someone else. "All the times he didn't know something. All the times he wasn't fair. Do you want me to show you Jane's list?"

Mrs. Tilley chewed her bottom lip. "I think not."

She said it so gently, Bonnie laughed. "We should do a revolution on him."

Mrs. Tilley laughed with her. "Oh, revolutions are for extreme circumstances." She put the leftover copies of the Declaration into her briefcase and snapped it closed. "I tell you what. I'll speak to . . . well, why not to Mrs. Atkins? She's in charge of the math sequence. I'll speak to her about it. Now, I have to get along. Thank you for a lovely day."

The bad thing, Bonnie thought as she walked home, was that Mrs. Tilley hadn't seemed surprised at the truth about Mr. Locke. The deep-down truth about Mr. Locke was, Bonnie realized, what she had said: Mr. Locke really didn't care.

That night, as they went over her homework, her father told Bonnie that during a conference with Schaffer's teacher, he had mentioned that sixth grade math was disappointing, that Bonnie wasn't getting the instruction she needed.

"Mrs. Atkins," he said, "has a lot of influence in the school. I'm sure she'll be able to do something.'

Bonnie nodded. She didn't believe anything would change.

6

Something's Weird

On a Monday morning, about a week later, Bonnie learned what Mrs. Atkins was doing about sixth grade math.

"I went into third grade after school," Shawna told the group as they stood on the grassy field, waiting for the bell, "to get my sister's homework. Mr. Locke was there, and our math was all over the board. She's teaching him how to teach it."

"Not that it's doing any good," said Jane. She looked around the playground. "Something's weird." There were no teachers outside; rather, two parents were on duty.

"Isn't it time?" Lucy Ann called from where she was standing with her friends.

"Five minutes ago," Nancy called back.

"I'm going to ask," Lucy Ann said. They watched her go across to one of the parents. The second graders' shrieks seemed extra loud, their games seemed to spin ever faster. "She said in a few minutes," Lucy Ann reported. "She said we'd be called. Something's weird."

When the bell finally rang, the children moved in quickly. In her classroom, Bonnie found Mr. Locke standing by a window, waiting. Without being told, the class sat. When the loudspeaker made the slight crackling that preceded Miss Cherry's announcements, there was very little quieting to be done.

"Good morning, dear children. This is Mrs. Atkins. I have a sad announcement to make. Our beloved principal, Miss Cherry, has passed away. She suffered a heart attack at nine o'clock last evening.

"Miss Cherry was devoted to her school and to her children. I know she would have wanted us to go on with our morning program, persevering toward those goals of educational excellence and personal growth to which she herself was dedicated. I'm sure we will each dedicate today's tasks to her memory."

Bonnie looked around. No one was crying. Are you supposed to cry right away when someone dies? she wondered.

Mrs. Atkins continued: "The superintendent has asked me to serve as acting principal until an interim principal is elected by the PAT next month. The Board of Education will appoint a permanent principal at the first of the year. A notice explaining this will go home to your parents.

"I'm honored to take up this sad duty. I assure

my third graders that I will continue with my classroom duties, as well.

"Before we begin our work, we will share a moment of silence in Miss Cherry's memory. The teachers have left the classroom doors open, so all the school can be as one. Will you stand, please?"

Mrs. Atkins's last words echoed down the halls. Bonnie could hear chairs scraping as everyone stood, could hear the unusual sound of over two hundred people being quiet together.

However, she had some trouble keeping her mind on Miss Cherry, that little-known, little-loved figure of the halls. For the whole long moment, all she could think was: Now I know someone who died!

When the moment of silence was over, Mr. Locke repeated Mrs. Atkins's thought: "I know Miss Cherry would want us to keep on with our regular schedule. Later, I'll give you time to write letters of condolence to Miss Cherry's family."

"During math, we hope," muttered Gail, who was suddenly standing by Bonnie's desk. She tossed down a packet of mimeographed pages and was gone.

The first few pages were folded back, and Bonnie saw that certain words had been circled in green ink: "Every member of the school community may participate in such a special election."

The rest looked equally uninteresting. Bonnie turned to the first page. The title was: "Board of Education: Bylaws."

"Bylaws!" Bonnie's head whipped around.

Gail was staring at her, her lips making a sign that might mean "Shhh!" and might mean "See?" and might mean "Wait!"

Bonnie slipped the bylaws under her science book and tried to study, although she completely forgot to dedicate her task to Miss Cherry's memory. Her mind was full of racing, tumbling thoughts.

Bonnie Mann did not believe in supernatural forces. Beyond a little pleasant daydreaming of winged horses racing over the ocean waves or of inheriting a fortune, she had had no inclination to consider the fantastic, till now. But now! Had Gail known Miss Cherry was going to die? Why had two people as different as Mr. Lipchik and Gail given her copies—which she had no interest in reading— of the Board of Education bylaws?

When the bell rang for recess, Bonnie went quickly to the door, then called loudly back to Jane and Nancy, "I'll be down in a minute. I have to wash my hands."

"I don't get it," she said, after Gail's scowl had sent the last fourth grader rushing from the girls' room. Bonnie leaned against the big brass radiator by the window. She could hear the shouts of children playing in the yard.

"They *elect* the interim principal," Gail said. "*All* members of the community can participate. *Kids* can vote. *You* can run."

"For principal?"

"For interim principal, not for long. When you win, you fire Locke."

Bonnie giggled. "A kid can't fire a teacher. They must have a law about it."

"There's no law; I'm sure of that."

"Gail, did you know"—Bonnie could hardly say it—"that Miss Cherry was going to die? You had everything all ready."

"I was only ready," Gail said, "in case. Like with that class chart. The PAT . . . What does that stand for, anyway?"

" 'Your Parents, Administrators, and Teachers, Standing Together for Excellence in Education.' " Bonnie had heard the slogan a hundred times.

Gail nodded. "The PAT sends all new parents copies of the bylaws. My parents don't care, so I read them. I always read everything, in case. That's how I found this great sentence: "Every member of the school community may participate. . . .'"

"It's impossible," Bonnie said.

"It's possible. The school board picks a *permanent* principal starting January first; and the superintendent chooses the *acting* principal for now—that's Mrs. Atkins. But the school community elects the *interim* principal, for in between the acting and the permanent, and that's you. And that's possible."

"Well, even if it's possible, it's crazy."

Gail shrugged. "I don't write the stupid bylaws.

I just know how to read them. Why do they bother to elect an interim principal at all for only a few weeks? That's *really* stupid. It might help us, though—maybe not many parents will think it's important to come vote."

"Gail? Did you talk with Mr. Lipchik about this?"

"Why would I talk to him? He's the custodian." Gail clicked her pen points in and out impatiently.

Bonnie splashed cold water on her face. There were no paper towels, so she grabbed some toilet paper and made faces into it as she dried off. Help! she thought. I'm stuck in the girls' room with a raving nut! "Well, why me? Bobby would . . ."

"No. *Not* Bobby," Gail said. "Look, don't take this as a total insult, but you're a really good kid. You're never rude, and you're helpful, and all the grown-ups trust you. They would never suspect."

Here it is again, Bonnie thought. Being good is messing up my life! Of course, this might be a chance to not be so good—although that was exactly what made her uneasy about Gail's plan. "How about if I just help? Why don't you run? You have a lot of ideas."

"I wouldn't have a chance," Gail said. "We have to get all the kids, even kindergarten, to vote for our candidate. They know you."

"Kindergarten kids? At a PAT election?"

"We'll need every vote. That's why we need a good, safe kid like you."

Bonnie went into one of the stalls to get away from Gail's intense eyes. She leaned against the door to hold it closed.

"We'll only have about five weeks," Gail's voice was grim. "We can't let anyone know you're running for real, till as late as possible. We don't want the grown-ups to get organized and campaign hard, or change the bylaws so kids can't vote. We shouldn't let them know we're serious till election night."

"Gail! You couldn't get a kid even nominated."

"First, it *is* legal," Gail said confidently. "The bylaws say the school community participates, but they don't say who the school community is. The school community has to include the children, right?"

"I don't know if they think so, all the parents . . ."

"Without us, they don't *have* a school. If every kid gets a stomachache the same morning and stays home, they'll find out who the school community is!"

Bonnie quickly flushed the toilet, so Gail wouldn't hear her laugh.

"No. We'd better not do that," Gail said. "They'd know how organized we are."

Bonnie came out and looked Gail straight in the eye. "You're serious, aren't you? You have an exact plan. You've been plotting this whole thing!"

At that moment, the fifth-grade Grimmet and her

best friend came in. The Grimmet washed her hands thoroughly both before and after she used the toilet, but Bonnie and Gail washed theirs longer. Finally, the Grimmet and her friend went to the door. "Remember, Bunnie: No staying in the girls' room during recess," the Grimmet said. "Miss Cherry says."

"Miss . . . Cherry . . . ?" Gail asked.

The fifth graders gasped and were gone.

"Bunnie!" said Bonnie.

"I bet Mrs. Atkins is going to run for principal," Gail said. "She'd never fire Locke. She'd just keep trying to teach him how to teach and say she's working on it. Yeah, I have a plan: We get Locke to help."

"Why would he help if your plan is to get him fired?"

"He won't get fired till after he helps get you elected."

"Wouldn't that be dirty? Pretending?"

"Isn't what he's doing dirty? Pretending to be a teacher?"

Wow! Bonnie thought. Wow! To say that. "Well, but Gail—how could I even be a principal and be a kid, too, in my classroom?"

"Don't worry," Gail said, clicking her pen to change colors and making a note. "It's only for a few weeks."

Bonnie thought this question shouldn't be ignored, but before she could go on, Gail was talking again.

"I'll suggest the idea to Locke for an American history project. In my old school, we did something like that. Not for real, but I could tell him how it worked. He can go to the teachers and the PAT for us. They won't worry about anything he suggests. Then, if we win, we'll really win, because it's all legal."

Bonnie felt she was drowning in Gail's flood of ideas. She tried to think of reasons why it wouldn't work. "But it's not right, a kid being principal."

"Who knows school better than a kid? You don't know budgets or how to order supplies or about the curriculum, but that's what's so great about this plan: All that stuff is done for this year. You just have to change things a little. Like fire Locke."

The idea of everyone voting for her had begun to feel terrific to Bonnie. She imagined being interviewed on television and kids applauding. She imagined telling everyone how everything should be. But Gail's last words stopped her. "That's not such a little thing, firing Mr. Locke."

Gail grinned. "It's the whole point."

"But what could I say? Why?"

"For not teaching math."

"He has a math class, every day. Almost every day."

"That's not teaching! Remember how upset you were after eight times zero? Remember!"

"Poor Mr. Locke."

"Don't think like that!" Gail said. "What about poor Jerry? What about all the poor kids who are stuck sitting listening to his confusion and getting yelled at and insulted? Don't feel sorry! He's wasting your sixth grade!"

Bonnie was relieved to hear the bell.

"Tell me tomorrow," Gail said. "You're not the only one who could do it. Just, you have the best chance."

Bonnie walked slowly back to her classroom among the boisterous, red-cheeked fourth graders racing in from the playground. She took her math homework from among the worksheets she had filled out the night before. She looked once more at the confusing lesson. She pulled out a NASA pencil, knowing even a NASA pencil wouldn't help.

"Where were you?" Jane said as she plopped into the next seat. "We needed you! We played in Bobby's game!"

"Seven of us," Nancy said, from Bonnie's other side. "Four of them. We *didn't* win." She matched Jane giggle for giggle.

It would have been so easy to just stick with my friends, Bonnie thought, instead of spending the whole stupid recess in the stupid girls' room talking stupid nonsense. She saw that Gail was once again writing intently into her pad.

"Did you hear?" Jane said. "Shawna's mom changed her mind again; she won't let us have the party." She opened her book. "Back to mindless math with mindless Mr. Locke. Sometimes I think this whole year is a waste."

Bonnie shivered at the echo of Gail's words.

7

Shocking Thoughts

Bonnie came home still wondering whether it would be good or bad to run for principal, wondering whether it might not *be* good to be bad, wishing she didn't have to decide. Schaffer soon gave her plenty of distraction.

He slammed in the front door, then slammed his books onto the hall table. When several papers from his notebook drifted to the floor, he left them there. He took his soccer ball to the head of the basement stairs and kicked it down.

"Schaffer? *What* is *wrong*?"

"Well . . . Is Mom home?"

"She's up in Dad's study, typing."

"They changed it again! Now we *can't* use the grassy field after school. Only the big kids. We're not having any kind of practice. And for P.E., we had to do jumping jacks and jump rope the whole time. We need a real coach, for soccer."

"Did you talk to Mrs. Atkins about it?"

"She said she'd try to work something out." Schaffer slammed himself into a chair. "Last week she said that." He was up again, opening the refrigerator. "Also, I'm sick of 'Put your hands on your desks and your head on your hands.' She loves that one."

Bonnie remembered what her father had said about Mrs. Atkins's good influence. "She's strict, but you learn a lot from her."

"I already know a lot." He slammed the refrigerator door, then grabbed open a cabinet and took a handful of peanuts. "All the people who think Mrs. Atkins is so great have already *done* third grade. They're out of there." He ran down the basement steps. "You can't trust anybody!"

Bonnie waited. When he came up again, carrying his ball, she asked, "Schaffer? Do you trust me?"

"Sure. A little. But what could you do?" He walked out of the house.

Bonnie picked up the mess of notebook pages in the front hall. She smiled, remembering Mrs. Tilley once teasing Bobby Roberts that his loose-leaf notebook was "considerably more loose of leaf than the manufacturers intended."

Bonnie put Schaffer's notice about the PAT election with her own. She didn't want her parents to see it till she knew what she would do.

She mixed leftover guacamole salad with leftover tuna salad and heaped this on half a bagel and half an English muffin. As she ate, her eye fell on the long list her parents kept on the refrigerator door of all the work to be done around the house. Some jobs had wages attached to tempt her and Schaffer. Bonnie noticed a new item: "Paint backyard chairs, *neatly*, $2. Use any old paints in basement."

Bonnie decided to get to that job before Schaffer did. She loved to paint.

Within half an hour, Bonnie had remembered that she always *thought* she loved to paint—and that it always turned out she hated it.

Her scheme of alternate blue and red legs and arms, rungs and slats, was a chaos of drips and uneven lines. Her own arms and legs were also partly red and blue, but in a less consistent pattern. Her skin itched wherever paint had stuck, and goose bumps rose as the afternoon grew cooler. From time to time, a dry crab apple leaf fell from the tree, touched drying paint, and fell no farther. Bonnie began to despair of ever getting out of the mess she kept making worse.

She was soon in such a foul mood that when she heard, "Afternoon!" and turned to see Mr. Lipchik leaning over the alley fence, her response was, "I hate Tom Sawyer!"

Mr. Lipchik smiled. "What's Tom Sawyer ever done to you?"

"He fooled me, again. Remember when he painted that fence? Every time, I think it's going to be so much fun."

"Books will give you all kinds of bad ideas, no doubt about it," Mr. Lipchik said. "Would you like some help?"

"Would you?" Bonnie could hardly believe his generous offer.

"If you have another brush . . . ?"

The extra brushes were already sticky beyond use, so Bonnie went inside to get another. She found her mother rummaging rather desperately in the freezer.

"Mr. Lipchik, from school, said he would help me paint. Okay?"

"Lucky you!" Mrs. Mann said, and went to the window to call hello to Mr. Lipchik.

When Bonnie came out again, she found him studying the drips and smudges. Tactfully, he said nothing about them, just lowered his lumpy knapsack to the ground beside the old wooden radio he had been carrying. "I saw a moving truck in front, up the block," he explained. "I figured there'd be some worthwhile trash out back. Got this radio. Got some books."

He went to work. Occasionally, just occasionally and very nicely, he gave Bonnie a bit of advice, and once he asked what her name was. For the most part, they painted in a companionable silence, and Bonnie's mind at last drifted back to Gail's proposal.

Would Mr. Lipchik be the person to talk with about her problem? Was it coincidence that he had come by today? Or did he already know? She tried a few questions, as a kind of test. "Did you know Miss Cherry would die?"

"No! She looked fine the last time I saw her, a week or two ago." He stopped painting to look at her. "Do you miss Miss Cherry?"

Bonnie wondered guiltily, Should I miss Miss Cherry? "Well, she was hardly there, you know, even when she was there."

"True," he said. "True. Mrs. Atkins ran the school, even then."

Bonnie looked directly into his mild blue eyes. "Well, are you a friend of Gail Dewksbury's?"

He shook his head. "She that new teacher?"

"No, the new girl in my class."

"Now whose room are you in, did you say?"

"Mr. Locke's."

"That big, stiff girl?" Bonnie nodded. "No, I've never met her."

"Gail has a copy of those bylaws, too. Those by-laws you gave me?"

"Did I? Why?"

"Okay," Bonnie said. "Mr. Lipchik, this is my problem. There's going to be an election for the new principal. Gail asked me to run. Do you think I should?"

Mr. Lipchik brushed carefully, evenly, along a chair slat. Finally he nodded sadly. "Might be a good idea. Things will certainly get worse, now, as she begins to feel her power." His voice rose. "Mrs. Atkins knows I keep that building going and she knows I study history, but whenever she sees me reading, she finds something that doesn't need doing for me to do instead. The woman is a threat to sustained concentration! I wonder she calls herself a teacher."

After this burst of passion, Bonnie waited a minute, then asked, "Well, do you think a kid could get elected principal?"

"Realistically?" He sucked on his cigar. "No. But history teaches that being realistic is not always realistic. People like to muck around where they don't belong. If men will fly to the moon, where they have no business whatsoever, a child could certainly be a principal here on earth."

"Most people wouldn't believe it could happen."

"People believe what they want to. If they want you to be principal, they'll believe it could happen, and they'll vote for you."

"Gail thinks it could happen. She really does." Bonnie explained the plan, then got to the heart of her worry: "But wouldn't it be . . . bad? Kids trying to do what the grown-ups should be doing?"

"Didn't you and I talk about this? Weren't you the one wanting to try not being so good?" Bonnie nodded. "Anyway, who's to say about bad? History teaches it's often necessary to be bad, by society's lights, to accomplish any good."

He stopped painting and looked at her. "No, I'd say the only question is: Are you prepared to be bad enough to do some good? Tell me, exactly what are your complaints about that school?"

"D-W is mostly pretty boring . . ." she began.

"You won't get far with that!" he snorted. "Schools are meant to be boring. Otherwise, why would anyone graduate and start doing the world's work? Boring was policy in my day, I expect it's policy now. What else?"

"Well, they don't teach us much, much that's . . ."

"Much that's real and useful?" Bonnie nodded. "Nothing new there, either," he said. "One day playing hooky with my friend Samuel was worth a month of school for me, as far as real education. Worth a year of school, as far as entertainment. That's why I left."

"Filling in those worksheets all the time!" Bonnie blurted out.

"Whoa, now!" Mr. Lipchik said. "Those worksheets may not be fun, but they are certainly real. Why, the Board of Education requires the poor teachers to do exactly the same. They fill in forms, put their checkmarks in the little boxes, make reports, on and on with this and that, just like you. Paperwork by the trashcanful. You should see the paper I cart away every quarter. File some, trash some. I doubt you can build an effective case on worksheets not being real."

He was up, removing leaves and brushing over

the scars they had left in the drying paint. "Have you other complaints?"

Bonnie took a deep breath. "Mr. Locke is it. He's mean and he's unfair and he doesn't teach math. Hardly at all! And when he does teach it, sometimes he gets it wrong."

"Why that's it!" Mr. Lipchik shouted. "There you have it! The man is an imposter! He's being paid to teach a subject, and he's not teaching it?"

"Yes!"

"The scalawag is taking the public's tax monies under false premises! As a student of history and the American political process, I guarantee you: There's your platform! There's your votes!"

"I guess he is a scalawag," Bonnie said, and tested the word again: "Scalawag! You don't feel safe when your teacher isn't right."

"An anarchy of untrue facts loosed upon the world! Do you know that man throws his peanut butter and mayonnaise crusts in the wastebasket, unwrapped? Sticky plum pits, too, never mind the mess it makes for me. But that's not a vote getter, I suppose. Better stay with the misuse of public funds."

"Mr. Lipchik, you're like a regular grown-up, worrying about the taxes of it."

"I am a grown-up, and I pay my taxes, and you'll need grown-ups' votes to win." He rolled his cigar between his fingers and gave a small, grown-up's laugh.

"I've heard some of the teachers talking about Mr. Locke," he went on. "Miss Camp, and Mrs. Tilley, and that teacher who works on the children one at a time in that little room. No respect. But there's not much they can do, is there? But you *do* have an idea. I'd say you were smart to do whatever you must to save yourselves, up to and including the drastic step of running for public office."

"But . . . how about me? I'd miss so many classes. I'd get behind."

"From what you say, you're getting behind now. Besides, I expect there's a world of education in being principal. Writing all those notices, adding up the absences, learning how to say no to everyone. Increase your vocabulary of long and solemn words. Oh, you'll learn a lot more than they usually teach in elementary school."

"You think I should do it?"

"Politics . . . ?" Mr. Lipchik thought for a moment. "Not a course I would recommend lightly to a friend. But perhaps you must. Grab the opportunity when it comes your way. A great general and my own personal hero, Ulysses S. Grant, said once: 'The readiness is all.' "

"Didn't Benjamin Franklin say that? Mrs. Tilley quoted . . ."

"Even the best teachers make mistakes. You must stay on guard. No, the school might well be better off with you as principal. . . ."

"What about . . . ? The worst is . . ." Bonnie's

voice was down to a whisper. "If I get elected, I'd have to fire Mr. Locke."

"You see? That's something else you'd learn. There's few people know how to fire someone decently."

"Mr. Lipchik! I'd have to fire my own teacher!"

"Shocking thought."

"Well, it is!"

"As shocking as a teacher who doesn't teach?"

Once again, Bonnie thought Mr. Lipchik sounded very much like Gail. "Besides," she said slowly, "it's not just for the sixth grade—there's other things I could do. . . ."

"You sound as if you mean to do it."

Bonnie gave a gulp, and then a grin, and then a very small nod.

"So. I'd better get on home. I have some nice pears and a tomato ripening for dinner." Mr. Lipchik stood to put on his knapsack. "You can handle the rest. Afternoon."

Bonnie looked with pleasure at the smoothly painted chairs. "Thank you! For talking and painting and everything! Good-bye." She walked to the back fence to watch him leave. There was not a spot of paint on him. On herself, of course, the mess remained.

8

Of All the Things
You Could Ever Be

At breakfast the next morning, after Schaffer had left for school, Bonnie gave her parents Mrs. Atkins's notice.

"Well, she's going to run." Mrs. Mann handed the paper to Mr. Mann. "I know campaign literature when I see it."

"She practically ran the school, anyway," Mr. Mann said. "It's a good little school. I'll vote for her."

Bonnie knew that with her often-distracted parents it was useful later, when the questions came, to be able to say "But I told you!" Also, she didn't know how soon news about the project would get out, and she wanted them to hear it from her. So she forced herself to ask, "How about voting for your daughter?" She explained the sixth-grade election project, though not how serious the effort would be.

"Marvelous!" Mrs. Mann said. "What a neat idea!"

"Mr. Locke is getting into some interesting work with you," Mr. Mann said. "I'm not sure I would have expected it of him."

Mrs. Mann kissed the top of Bonnie's head as they all got up from the table. "This is a difficult time for us, Bon. Now the primary's won, I've got to rewrite our material for the general election. And Dad's launch is getting closer. I'm sure Mrs. Atkins has things in hand, but keep your ears open and tell us anything we should know. It's wonderful about you running in the mock election."

Bonnie looked at her parents' vague and loving faces and smiled and left for school.

Gail was at the corner waiting for Bonnie's answer. Gail immediately began making plans: "We need a small group of kids to work with us."

"A steering committee," Bonnie said.

"A steering committee," Gail repeated. "Your mother's in politics, isn't she? Is she a campaign manager?"

"Something like that," Bonnie said. "I try not to notice."

"You'd better tune in now. You might get some ideas." Gail pulled out her chart of the sixth grade. "We need someone from each group."

"I don't know if they could all work together," Bonnie said. "We have a good class, but . . . Lucy Ann goes to movies with eighth grade boys!"

"Yes, but if we have the leader of each group with us, when it's time to tell the class we really mean it, they can each convince their own friends. So, you and Bobby and Lucy Ann. Jerry?"

Bonnie nodded. "Jerry's friends with lots of kids in other classes."

"And me," Gail said. "That's probably enough."

"We should have Jane," Bonnie said. "She knows a lot of little kids, because of her brothers and baby-sitting. Also, she's been organizing a boy/girl party. Jane's fabulous on lists."

"Lists?"

"Politics is mostly lists," Bonnie said, "as far as I can see. You make lists."

"Okay," Gail said. "Jane."

"Gail, do you really think we could beat Mrs. Atkins?"

"We have a chance. Maybe not many parents will come vote, if they don't know it's a real election. They probably think everything's fine. Why do they keep calling it a 'good little school'?"

"My dad does that."

"All they mean is the kids behave. That's all they mean."

Something clicked for Bonnie: *That* was why those report cards about being so cooperative had begun to bother her!

"Anyway," Gail was saying, "I don't want to go to a 'good little' school. I want my school to be Great! Huge! Terrific!" With each adjective, Gail made a stiff-legged leap onto another sidewalk square.

Bonnie laughed as she picked up the books Gail was dropping. "You know, most kids haven't ever voted about anything real."

"When we get the steering committee going, we'll figure out what the kids care about, so we can convince them."

"Schaffer cares about no soccer coach and dumb P.E."

"Yes," Gail said. "That's a good issue." They were near school now, children were running by, and she lowered her voice. "I'll talk to Locke at recess and get things started. You get those kids to meet us, by the high rock, after school."

The others all said they would come, though Bonnie told the truth only to Jane, after lunch, in a far corner of the grassy field.

"You ninny!" Jane cried out. "Of all the things you could ever be, why would you ever want to even pretend to be principal?"

Bonnie tried to think of a Jane kind of reason. "So I can hear what the teachers say in the teachers' lounge?"

"Good! And tell your best friend."

"I'm sorry, my dear, but it *may* be confidential!" Bonnie giggled. "Also so I can always have important business at eleven and miss math."

"You should always make a long loudspeaker announcement at eleven and rescue us all. Good, Bon! This'll be fun!"

"Jane. This is serious." Bonnie shivered. "I'm supposed to fire Mr. Locke."

"You mean it's really real?"

Bonnie nodded.

"I can't believe you would do that. Do you believe it?"

"I think so."

"Nobody would believe it," Jane said. "That's so serious! Are you going to get kicked out of school? Do your parents know?"

"I told them pretty much of it, but they don't exactly know."

"You're going to fire Mr. Locke?"

"I have to. That's why Gail's doing it."

"Big Gail thinks she's the boss of everything! Bon? Why don't you just tell Mrs. Atkins about Mr. Locke and let her take care of it?"

"My dad already did. So did Mrs. Tilley. That's why she's tutoring him. If anything's going to *happen*, *we* have to do it."

I can't believe it, Bonnie thought. I can't believe I'm saying this. But she couldn't tell even Jane how scared she was, starting to be so bad.

Jane's voice was suddenly chirping and gay: "And then you'll get us a new teacher! Will you get us a pretty one? One who will smile?"

"What I have to get is someone who can teach. And who won't pick on Jerry. And Gilly, and Michael Burney, and . . ."

"He picks on the whole class," Jane said. "He just

waits his chance for each person. Well, good idea, Bon. But . . . why doesn't Bobby run?"

"Jane! I thought you were my friend! Nobody asked him, that's why. It's Gail's idea, and she asked me, and the reason is: I have a better chance to win."

"No offense, Bonnie, but Bobby wins everything. Bobby's the one who . . . wins."

Bonnie couldn't stand to talk again about how good she was. "Gail will explain it. She has it all organized."

But the meeting was very disorganized.

"Why do we have to have a meeting?" Lucy Ann asked, refusing to sit on the high rock that stood behind the playground, or on any of the smaller boulders nearby. "After we've sat all day in stupid school."

"I can't stay long," Bobby said. "I'm going to Walter's."

Jerry rested the abandoned shell of a cicada on Jane's shoe. Jane, who had three younger brothers, simply flicked it off. When Jerry tried Lucy Ann's shoe, he was rewarded with a proper squeal. He scampered up the high rock, placing his feet and hands in the many cracks on its sloping face.

"In a day or two," Gail said, loudly, "Mr. Locke is going to announce a new project."

"Whoopee," said Lucy Ann. "Life in Mr. Locke's class is just one fantastic thrill after another."

"He's going to add four and four and see if he can

get it right?" Jerry jumped from the top. "Amazing!"

Bonnie was glad it was Gail's job to convince the others.

"The project," Gail said, "is for our American history class to run a candidate in the PAT election for interim principal."

"For this we hang around all afternoon and get our toes friz?" Lucy Ann asked.

"There's a good chance," Gail said, using the teacher's trick of talking more softly in order to command attention, "that if this group of class leaders works together," and here she looked around soberly, implying that class leaders didn't throw moss at each other, "we really can elect a sixth grader principal of Daniel Webster."

In the sudden silence, she added: "The first thing our new principal will do is fire the worst sixth-grade teacher ever, Stuart Locke."

There were cheers then, but the cheers soon changed to "We couldn't!" and "A kid can't be principal."

"Okay, I don't think that's legal," Bobby said. "Legally."

Gail opened her copy of the bylaws and explained how a student could, and should, and would, run and be elected.

"So who would be the candidate?" Lucy Ann asked. "Bobby?" She smiled sideways at him, but Bobby was looking modestly at his boots.

"Bonnie," Gail said.

Bobby looked up, entirely confused.

In the whole campaign, Bonnie had no moment more embarrassing than this, when she seemed to be challenging Bobby Roberts's natural place as, simply, the greatest kid in the class.

"Gee, I like Bonnie," Jerry said. "But wouldn't more little kids vote for Bobby?"

Once again, Bobby Roberts contemplated his boots.

"Bobby wins too much," Gail said. "If we ran him, the grown-ups might realize what we're doing. We need to keep everyone thinking this is just a pretend class project till the last minute." Gail smiled at Bobby. "Even Mrs. Atkins would be afraid if Bobby ran against her." Bonnie was relieved to see Bobby smile modestly back.

"So why Bonnie?" Lucy Ann asked.

"Bonnie's cooperative and all that stuff. Everyone likes her, and no one would be afraid of her." Not for the first time, Bonnie felt Gail's compliments were not exactly complimentary.

Lucy Ann still had doubts. "Isn't D-W supposed to be a good school?"

"Maybe it's not so good," Gail said. "Maybe it's like the emperor's new clothes. No clothes, but nobody admits it, till a kid tells the truth."

"Walter has a friend who goes to Dewey," Bobby said. "They use the same math book, and they're already on chapter five."

"If D-W is so good, why is the best thing recess?"

Bonnie spoke at last, her voice a high, nervous squeak. "Why is school so boring? Going so slow down the chapter questions till every kid gets every answer? The horrible lunchroom? P.E. that's just running around. All those things, not just Mr. Locke. Waiting for the projector to work? Remember awful second grade? Why don't they ever teach us what we want to know? Remember when Mr. Locke wasn't there, and Mrs. Tilley was? That's how good school can be."

"But it's not right," Lucy Ann said. "We're the kids."

"If I'm going to be a veterinarian," Gail said, "I need good math and good science. Letting him waste my whole year, that's what's not right, Lucy Ann. That's stupid."

Bonnie could feel the others grow uneasy. She knew they didn't quite trust Gail. They moved over the face of the high rock, picking at lichen, picking at moss. None of them had yet agreed to join the campaign.

Gail's bossy ways made Bonnie uncomfortable, too. But she liked what she herself had said. She trusted the look in Bobby's eyes as he thought about having a good teacher again.

9

Small Mammals
and Other Issues

"Are you Bonnie?"

Bonnie looked down from her lunchtime conversation with Gillian and Jane on Friday and saw a small boy pulling on the edge of her jacket. It was the kindergarten Grimmet, no doubt about it. He had on the kindergarten uniform of high black sneakers, jeans, and a jacket buttoned around his neck for a Batman cape. He had the adorable Grimmet face. Two other little boys stood behind him.

"I'm Bonnie."

"Bonnie?"

"Yes?"

"If you was the principal?"

"Yes?"

"Could the kindergarten have a rabbit *and* a guinea pig?"

"What did Miss Everts say?"

"She says we have to choose." "She says we have to vote." All three boys were suddenly, angrily, engaged in the conversation. "She says we are democracy."

"Can't you vote to have both?"

"Only which." "Rabbit or." "She doesn't like the smell." "She doesn't want to clean up so much poop."

"With both," the Grimmet said, "you learn more. "We'll clean up the poop." "Jeremy likes cleaning poop."

All three boys turned to look across the yard. Bonnie wondered which spaceship was Jeremy.

"Also, two kids get to hold at the same time."

The candidate, herself fond of cuddling small mammals, took a stand: "If I am principal, the kindergarten can vote to have a rabbit *and* a guinea pig."

"Good." The kindergarten Grimmet nodded, and the three raced back across the playground.

"Bonnie!" Gillian jumped around in a circle, waving her hands. "Bonnie, that was excellent! You got three votes!"

"*If* those little kids even get to the PAT meeting," Jane said.

"Bonnie! I bet you get their whole classful of votes!" Gillian was still spinning. "I love campaigning!"

As Gillian and Jane chattered on, Bonnie wondered if a principal was allowed to tell a teacher she had to have both a guinea pig and a rabbit. Was there a principal's handbook that gave information like that?

The fifth-grade Grimmet passed close behind her then, walking arm in arm with her best friend. ". . . stupid project . . ." the Grimmet said in a very loud whisper. ". . . think they're so great . . ."

Bonnie, pretending not to hear, looked out at the running, jumping, yelling, whispering children in the school yard. On one of the first cold days of fall, the colors of new jackets and mittens and hats were fresh and clear. The third-grade girls huddled in a tight group; awed kindergarteners watched big girls jumping rope. Although the October moon mission had come and gone, a few astronauts continued to blast off. Children were digging into a slope where grass no longer tried to grow, basketball games raged on the blacktop, and at the far end of the grassy field, five girls were inventing a dance. The many were pushing the lucky few who had found places on the tire swings, and a crowd of different ages gossiped upside down throughout the monkey bars.

Bonnie noticed the kindergarten Grimmet talking excitedly to six or seven of his classmates. For the first time she understood that each child was a separate person who would make up his or her own mind, for his or her own reasons, to vote or not to vote for Bonnie Mann.

That morning, in Friday assembly, class president Bobby Roberts had announced the "Experiment in

Democracy" to the school, and now the campaign was clearly under way.

All week, the setting up of the election project had gone smoothly. Bonnie's admiration for Gail had grown as every day, every recess, she seemed to have more good news.

"Locke likes the idea. He wants to call it 'Exercise in Democracy,'" Gail had told Bonnie at lunch on Tuesday. By Wednesday, everyone who was asked had agreed to be on the Steering Committee, and that afternoon the sixth grade was divided into committees. Gail planned that most of the organizing, research, making of campaign literature and posters, and other work would be done during Mr. Locke's American history class.

On Wednesday, too, Gail's Bylaws Committee had brought it to Mr. Locke's attention that children actually could vote in the election. On Thursday, Mr. Locke had mentioned this to Mr. Grimmet, who was president of the PAT. Mr. Grimmet had said, "Hey, that's kinda cute," and told that afternoon's meeting of the PAT executive committee about "the new twist to Mr. Locke's spiffy little 'Experience in Democracy.'" Mrs. Atkins, who had just been accepting congratulations on her own candidacy, smiled, though rather coolly. So everything was arranged, and on Friday the campaign began.

Bonnie never found out how Gail knew all this. Learning what went on at a PAT meeting was just one more reason, she thought, that it was great to be working with Gail.

She was not quite so admiring when Gail started organizing *her*. "Do you want some help with your speech?" she asked one day.

"My speech?" Bonnie asked.

"To the PAT meeting, election night."

"Speech?"

"Yes. That's what candidates do."

"Not me!"

"It only has to be for five minutes. Do you want a Speech Committee?"

"No!" Bonnie said, then more calmly, "No, thank you."

"Okay." Gail looked at Bonnie till Bonnie looked away. "But start thinking about what you want to say."

There was absolutely nothing Bonnie wanted to get up and say to the Parents, Administrators, and Teachers. Still, she knew that, once again, Gail was right. She comforted herself with the thought that the speech was more than four weeks away.

Meanwhile, she suffered other embarrassments.

One afternoon, Lucy Ann took Bonnie to the Big Room for an interview. Her Materials Committee was planning a leaflet listing the issues and giving information about the candidate.

"So," Lucy Ann asked, spreading her list of questions out on one of the long lunch tables, "what's your middle name?"

"You can't! I won't run if I have to tell! You don't need . . . !"

"Okay!" Lucy Ann said. "Well, what's your favorite snack?"

"Ah . . ." Bonnie said. "That's kind of embarrassing. My mother . . . Lucy Ann! That's not important for the election."

"Well, people like to know what people like to eat." Lucy Ann looked at her questions. "The fifth graders keep asking: If you're principal, how are you going to get educated? Missing class so much."

Bonnie had been worrying a lot about exactly this, and she wasn't sure she had a good answer, for Lucy Ann or for herself. "Well, Mrs. Atkins is principal now, and she's in with her class most of the time. So I probably won't have to miss much. You don't have to even mention it. Try another question."

"Are you dating yet?"

"Lucy Ann!"

"Bonnie! We have to say something interesting about you."

"Say I've been in D-W since kindergarten."

"So has the fifth-grade Grimmet, but I wouldn't vote for her."

"You know what?" Bonnie said. "Ask Jane. She knows what I eat and everything; whatever Jane says is okay."

*   *   *

"You can tell Lucy Ann all that stuff. You know all about me," Bonnie told Jane that evening.

The campaign was becoming a confusing mix of conversations with children Bonnie barely knew, Steering Committee meetings at the high rock, and the lingering feeling that she was doing something very bad, balanced by constant evidence from Mr. Locke that it was worth every risk. Her great comfort was in long phone calls with Jane.

"I don't know your middle name," Jane's voice had a hint in it.

"Lucky you," Bonnie said. "Listen, Jane. How am I going to *be* a principal? Lucy Ann asked me, and everybody asks. How am I going to do it? Like what if a parent calls up for a conference? What if a teacher wants to take a class to the zoo? Do I say yes or no?"

"I bet Miss Boyard does most of the principal's work, anyway," Jane said. Miss Boyard was the school secretary. "She's so nice, she'll tell you where the alarm is for fire drills and all that stuff. And I'm sure Mrs. Tilley would give you some tips."

"Maybe Miss Boyard would teach me to type! She's so fast!" Bonnie sighed. "I guess I can do most of the principal stuff before school and at recess."

"Sure. And if you're in class, Miss Boyard can talk to people who call. Let the kids' teachers do the talking at the conferences. Miss Cherry hardly opened her mouth, and everyone thought she was so important."

"What about my work? How am I going to find out my assignments?"

"I'll give you the ones you miss. We absolutely have to talk every night, anyway, so you can tell me who's bad and who's dumb and everything. And if you get stuck in the office and come late to class, you know you don't miss much, just getting settled and listening to the principal's stupid announcements. Ooops, sorry, your highness!"

"Watch it, Jane!"

"Listen, one thing, Bon. Shawna and Gilly and Nancy and I have decided: We are never, ever, not even if we get sent to the office, going to call you 'Miss Mann'!"

Bonnie giggled, but this reminded her of another worry: "What about the kids? They might think they can do anything, bring their radios to school and pop bubble gum all day and skip their homework."

"Be tough! Tell them they won't get a soccer coach if they mess around. Bobby and his guys will remind them. You can do it, Bon. And the principal jobs like walking fiercely in the halls, you don't want to do those, anyway."

"Gail says not to worry because it's only for a few weeks."

"All Gail cares about is getting people to do what she wants."

"Gail's good," Bonnie said. "She figures it all out. Nobody else is doing anything about Mr. Locke, not the parents, not the teachers."

"That doesn't mean I have to like her."

"What do your parents think? About it."

"They don't like it."

Bonnie felt a guilty shiver. She adored Jane's parents.

"They say if we have so much extra time, we should be using it for math. They don't understand at all."

A long silence made Bonnie fear Jane would hang up. She asked quickly, "Are you still working on the boy/girl party?"

"Sure! Hey, Bonnie?"

"Yes?"

"If you were the principal?"

"Yes?"

"Could we have boy/girl parties at school?"

"Jane, shut up."

"Bonnie? I'll vote for you? Pleeeeease?"

"Jane, shut up!"

"Bonnie?"

"What!"

"Can we have a boy/girl party *and* a guinea pig?"

"Where's Jerry?" Gail asked the others on the Steering Committee. "Again?"

"On the blacktop," Bobby said from the top of the high rock.

"He said to say he's campaigning with the kids in other classes."

"He's playing basketball, is what's he's doing. Someone go get him." Gail made a check in her notebook.

"You're doing attendance?" Lucy Ann asked. "On us?"

Jane rolled her eyes at Bonnie.

"She's right," Bonnie whispered. "It's better if everyone comes."

"Now," Gail said, glaring at Jerry as he ran up, "here are our issues so far: firing Mr. Locke; getting playground equipment that's not broken; getting a soccer coach; letting the kindergarten vote on a rabbit and a guinea pig."

" 'Bonnie's Little Zoo,' we're going to call it," Jane said.

"Listen, Jane," Bonnie said. "One of those picky little kindergarten kids who keeps bothering me is your brother."

"So?" Jane asked. "He has a right. This is a democracy, isn't it? This is a free country."

"Come on. Be serious," Gail said. "We need more issues."

"If we could fix the lunchroom?"

"If we could fix the lunchroom!"

About half the Ð-W children walked home for lunch, but the rest crammed into the Big Room to eat and, as Jane said now, "everybody turns into loud, messy, rude, disgusting monsters."

"Jerry, if your obnoxious little friends . . ." Lucy Ann said.

"Your whole table and those straws, last week . . ." Jerry answered.

"Remember in third grade?" Bonnie whispered to Jane. She loved to remember probably the worst thing she had ever done: She had written "Lucy Ann Smells" in lukewarm tomato soup across her table, and stuck raisins in it, and left it there.

"I wouldn't mention it right now," Jane whispered back.

". . . mashed grapes!" Lucy Ann was complaining loudly.

"Yeah, and we had to clean it up!" Bobby said.

Jerry sighed. "No one could fix that lunchroom."

Everyone believed him, and the Steering Committee went on to other issues.

"You know what I hate?" Lucy Ann asked. "I hate him drinking that coffee."

There was a growl of agreement.

"But he needs it," Jerry said. "He has to take a sip every time he doesn't know the answer. He needs about a gallon a day."

"It's not fair," Bonnie said. "He can have coffee, and we can't sneak even one peanut from our lunch."

"So, no eating in class, or if he can, we can," said Lucy Ann.

"No," Gail said. "That's not important enough for an issue."

"Let's say . . ." Bonnie thought for a minute. "The rules are for everyone. Fair rules."

"That would be okay," Gail said. "Also we need an issue for parents. Does anybody know something parents are mad about?"

"I sit for some second graders," Jane said. "Their parents say the kids can hardly write. They're worried about that."

"Next year with Mrs. Atkins, boy, they'll learn," Lucy Ann said.

Gail asked, "So how could we say we'd help the second grade?"

"Bonnie fires two teachers!" Jerry shouted. "Whammo!"

"We should save firing for our own teacher," Jane said. "We're doing all the work."

"Well, think about it," Gail said, and looked at her list. "Any ideas for our slogan?" There was silence. "Think, you guys! Bobby, tell about the voting."

Bobby explained that his Vote Analysis Committee was studying presidential elections according to the turnout of voters, and how the voter groups felt about certain issues.

"Huh?" said Jerry.

"Okay," Bobby said. "Like what if sixty percent of group A votes for candidate Y and eighty percent of group B votes for candidate Z, and A is twice as big as B and only half of B votes, but seventy-five percent of A votes? Like that."

Bonnie was appalled. Apparently math had its place in politics, too. Perhaps, she thought, there is no escape.

"Wait." Bobby flipped back and forth through the chaotic pages of his notebook. "Here. Say all the grown-ups vote for Mrs. Atkins and all the kids vote for Bonnie. Okay, and say each kid has two parents, so two to one in favor of them, but lots of families have more than one kid and some kids live with only one parent—so . . ."

"Huh?" said Jerry.

"Anyway," Bobby said, "it doesn't mean much because we don't know who will come to the meeting."

"Probably not many parents will come," Lucy Ann said. "It's such a dinky little election."

"Still we have to get every kid we can," Gail said. "Anything can happen—like if they find out about our plan. . . ."

"Even if a lot of kids come, they might not all vote for Bonnie," Jane said. "All those Grimmets and things."

"Don't worry about all those little kids," Lucy Ann said.

"A vote's a vote," Bonnie said. "In this election, a first grader's vote is going to count just as much as . . . as Mrs. Atkins's vote—the same, exactly!"

"That's so great!" said Jane.

"That's so cool!" said Bobby, picking up a stone and flinging it high and far.

"That's our only hope," said Gail. "Jane and I are working on setting up a Sitting Station, so lots of parents will bring their little kids."

"The only easy part of this whole election is fourth grade," Jerry said. "Fourth is all for Bonnie."

"Fifth is impossible," Lucy Ann said. "They think the election project is stupid. Anyway, the ones in spelling club love Mr. Locke. He's goody-goody nice to them, and they're goody-goody nice right back."

"Creepy-creepy, goody-goody fifth," said Jane. "If we could figure out how to get them to stay home, election night, and forever! . . ."

"That's the only thing we know for sure," Bobby said. "We need those fifth-grade votes."

"Bonnie? What's in your speech for the fifth graders?"

This was the second time Gail had asked about her speech in front of the others, like a teacher bawling her out about homework, Bonnie thought. "Nothing yet," she whispered.

"Haven't you started?"

"I've started!" Bonnie said, but she hoped she wouldn't have to show Gail the paper with just a few scratched-out words on it.

"Well, be sure there's something for the fifth. And put some quotes in it. Grown-ups love famous quotes."

Lucy Ann was shivering, hugging her jacket around her, tying and retying her scarf. "Can't we go?"

Jerry lay on top of the high rock, staring down at the game.

"Okay," Gail said. "For next time, figure out: a good slogan; how to fix the lunchroom; how to help the second grade write; how to get the fifth-grade vote. And come on time! And Bonnie—work on that speech!"

"I will," Bonnie said, so softly only she could hear. In the gloomy silence, as the others moved off, she could feel Jane looking at her, then looking away.

10

Down with
King George!

"Bonnie?" A week later, the kindergarten Grimmet, with two little boys behind, tugged on her jacket again.

"Yes?"

"If you was the principal?"

"Yes?"

"Could the kindergarten have two rabbits and two guinea pigs?"

"Would Miss Everts like so many?"

"No."

"Why do you want two?" Bonnie asked.

"It's more fun. And you learn more." The Grimmet looked behind him, and the two giggled. "And they have babies."

"We'll take care of them."

"Did you tell her that?"

"She says they stink weekends." "We'll clean them up, Mondays." "Bonnie? If you was principal?"

Bonnie felt her face mimicking an expression she had seen on her mother's, when she or Schaffer asked for still one more goody in the supermarket, or still one more guest for a birthday party, or still one more dive before coming out of the pool, asking and begging and giving reasonable reasons that made it harder for her mother to say no.

"Yes," Bonnie said. But while she was thinking of something stern to add so she would feel in control of the situation, the boys ran off.

This was just the beginning of a long and difficult day on the campaign trail. That morning, Jerry, chairman of the Budget and Fund-Raising Committee, asked Bonnie to come to other classrooms with him to announce the first bake sale. "So every kid will know you. For the sake of the famous Exercise in Democracy!"

"I can't!" Bonnie said. "It sounds so boasting. Like 'Buy your cupcake so the great me can be principal.'"

"It's not for you, Bonnie," Jane said. "Forget you. It's for all of us. Go!"

Mr. Locke gave permission, and soon Bonnie and Jerry were walking slowly through the pleasant halls, stopping to look at everybody's haiku outside fourth grade, and everybody's self-portrait outside second, and everybody's jack-o'-lantern story outside third.

The first-grade teacher asked them to wait a few moments since part of the class wasn't back from the library. Bonnie and Jerry walked around looking at the good old books in the reading corner and the cubbies decorated with animal cutouts. They tried to find anything at all alive in the fish tank and tried to recognize the shapes of colored clay drying on the broad windowsill.

"That one's mine," said a first grader, pointing.

"What is it?" Bonnie asked. "It's very pretty."

"It isn't pretty!" the child said. "It's a dinosaur."

"Oh, I see," Bonnie said. She picked up another piece of clay and asked another child, "Which is your dinosaur?"

"You got mine. It's not a dinosaur," the second child said, and said nothing more but continued to stare at Bonnie.

Bonnie looked from one nasty little child to the other. They both looked rather like Grimmets. They certainly acted like Grimmets. But she'd thought there weren't any Grimmets in first grade; she was sure there weren't *two*. Were the Grimmets multiplying? Were they taking over the school? She looked to Jerry for help, but he was simply grinning at her, waiting to see how she got out of this predicament.

Bonnie turned back to the hardened yellow puddle in her hand. "It's very"—she chose the safest word she could think of—"nice."

"It isn't nice!" the second child said. "It's a fried egg."

Bonnie swallowed her smile and put the fried egg carefully down. She looked very hard at Jerry.

"You all sure are creative," he said.

As they quickly moved to the front of the room, they heard a loud voice: "I don't know why she's trying to be the principal. She doesn't know anything about school!"

Escaping to the hall a few minutes later, and not at all ready to go into another class, Bonnie and Jerry walked aimlessly along, listening to the droning voices reading aloud, the murmurs of question and answer from the classrooms.

Then, like fresh air come sparkling into a stuffy room through an opened window, they heard the many noises of Mr. Lipchik coming down the hall. The wheels under his big gray trash can squeaked, the handles of the broom and mop rattled, and Mr. Lipchik whistled "Yankee Doodle."

He raised his hand to Bonnie in a significant gesture and stepped into a classroom to return a wastebasket.

"Does Mr. Lipchik know you?" Jerry asked.

"He's one of my campaign advisers," Bonnie said, delighted at her own words.

"I've decided your campaign is very important," Mr. Lipchik said rather gloomily when he joined them, "and I have an idea for you. This situation can't go on. You're after Locke, but she's . . . Uh-oh."

Mrs. Atkins had opened her door. She stood for a moment, staring her class completely quiet. Jerry grabbed Bonnie's hand and pulled her down behind the trash can. Bonnie's heart beat wildly as Mrs. Atkins stopped just a few feet away.

"Mr. Lipchik? Don't you usually do this noisy work at a more appropriate time, before or after school? If you wish to change your routines, you will check with me. Beforehand." Mrs. Atkins walked on toward the office.

"I've heard," Mr. Lipchik continued when she was out of sight, "your friends when they're plotting refer to . . . your opponent by name. There have been some close calls; if the teachers and parents learn what you're up to, that would be the end of it."

"Yes!" Bonnie said. "We'll tell them to be careful."

"You might," Mr. Lipchik went right on, "want to use a code name. That's been proven quite effective throughout history. Then you could talk about her openly."

"That's good!" Bonnie had noticed his eyes shining. "What name?"

"I don't like monarchies, however disguised, and we may as well be honest about what we have here. She's growing more royal every day. What would you think of 'King George'?"

"Excellent!" Bonnie laughed loud.

"Down with King George!" Jerry whispered.

"I thought of it yesterday when she asked me— when she told me—to wash her car. *En garde*," he whispered. "King George approaches."

He started his can rolling, and Bonnie and Jerry continued toward the second grade, barely looking at Mrs. Atkins as she passed.

Soon, however, they were stuck in her classroom for twenty minutes. It seemed like an hour.

They found the third graders uncomfortably still, and Mrs. Atkins standing by her desk, her elbows at her side and her hands clasped over her belt. She nodded to Bonnie and Jerry, then went on speaking:

"I was quite surprised to find this . . . original verse, with no name on it, among the very good papers I was correcting last evening. I was more than surprised at the poor taste in both language and subject matter."

The children looked at their desks as Mrs. Atkins's gaze passed over them. Bonnie saw Schaffer look down, then grin sideways at the third-grade Grimmet. The Grimmet was perilously close to the giggles. Luckily for him, Mrs. Atkins went sternly on.

"I will expect whoever was responsible for this poem to try his hand at a proper one, on the subject of romance, since that is his interest, to be handed in tomorrow, *with* his name on it. I will expect all writing assignments to be done with respect for your class, your school, and the English language. Misbehavior on paper is as inappropriate as misbehavior in class. Please excuse me for a moment."

Jerry and Bonnie thought she had paused for their

announcement, but they turned to see Miss Boyard smiling hello to them. The secretary was always a pretty sight, with her gray-blond curls piled high on her head, her bright jewelry and clothing, and her elegant high heels. Bonnie and Jerry smiled back, and the third graders relaxed, ready to enjoy what was clearly a familiar ceremony.

Bonnie watched Mrs. Atkins sit at her desk and Miss Boyard place some papers before her. Mrs. Atkins read each memo and letter from beginning to end. She took her purse from the bottom left-hand drawer and removed her private fountain pen, unscrewed the top, and tested the flow of ink. She signed her name and underlined each signature with a flourish, ending with arm, hand, and pen high in the air.

"King George" is right! Bonnie thought. She nudged Jerry and pointed to the Good Citizen sign: "We Pledge to: Be Cooperative. Follow School and Classroom Rules. Complete School, Class, and Homework on Time. Listen Well."

"Sounds like my report cards," Bonnie whispered.

"Sounds like Gail," Jerry whispered back.

Mrs. Atkins glanced up, and they whispered no more.

She covered her pen and put away her purse. "This will demonstrate the value of a clear and pleasing cursive writing style. If you have an important signature someday, I'm sure you will want it to lie gracefully upon the page." She patted the documents and nodded to Miss Boyard.

As Miss Boyard passed Bonnie and Jerry on her way out, they saw the slightest twitch of her mouth, the slightest roll of her eyes.

Mrs. Atkins turned. "Good afternoon, Bonnie, Jerry."

"Good afternoon, Mrs. Atkins," they said, and stepped forward.

"I'm sorry to keep you waiting, but you have caught us at an unfortunate moment. Class, because one person chose to write this unpleasant verse, we are all forced to have five additional spelling words for homework. Please take out fresh paper. I will give the word, the spelling, and the context.

"The words are: mischievous, reign, receive, science, neighbor. Mischievous. M-I-S-C-H-I-E-V-O-U-S. Tom Sawyer was a mischievous little fellow."

The room was absolutely still.

"Reign," Mrs. Atkins said. "R-E-I-G-N."

"Wow!" Jerry said, when he and Bonnie at last breathed the sweet air of freedom in the hall. "King George is pow-er-ful!"

"They all think Tom Sawyer is so cute," Bonnie said. "But if *we* do mischief! . . ."

"Yeah, lucky Tom," Jerry said. "He got famous for doing his."

"Do you think the kid who wrote the dirty poem will tell on himself?"

"Oh, sure," Jerry said. "I always did. I thought she could see what I was thinking, anyway, so I'd get it worse if I didn't."

"Did you write dirty poems to her?"

Jerry shook his head. "I wasn't that good."

"Like what then?"

"Gee. I did so many. Once my mother put carrot strips in my sandwich, so I gave it to the gerbil, and she didn't like it. Mrs. Atkins, I mean. The gerbil liked it pretty good. One time Spencer and I threw all the chalk out the window during lunch."

"I remember that one. That was you?"

"And Spencer. Once we hid the spelling workbooks in the boys' room. Remember Spencer?"

Bonnie nodded. They were back outside their own classroom, now, waiting to go in until Mr. Locke stopped bawling someone out.

"I wish he'd get a regular teacher's voice, like Mrs. Atkins or Mrs. Tilley," Bonnie said. "Jerry! If those kids think Mrs. Atkins can see what they're thinking, they'll never vote for anyone but her!"

"When you're in third, you think she's magic or something."

"How can we convince them it's a secret ballot and she could never know?" Bonnie stared through the glass into the sixth-grade room. Mr. Locke was still loudly annoyed about something. After a moment, she asked, "Is D-W a good little school?"

"I don't know," Jerry said. "Are the kids supposed to know?"

Bonnie and Jerry leaned their foreheads against the cool yellow tiles and talked softly, waiting for calm.

"That was my worst day of the whole campaign," Bonnie told Jane that night. "The awful kindergarten Grimmet again, the awful first graders, and awful, awful, awful Mrs. Atkins."

Jane reminded her of the two good parts: The naming of King George, and Jerry figuring out the answer to one of their biggest problems: how to make cheap campaign buttons. He suggested they use pieces of wide bandage tape decorated with fancy *B*s in colored ink. "I made my Bon-Daid as soon as I got home. I'm wearing it tomorrow. On my ankle."

"Jane, you don't wear campaign buttons on your ankle!"

"You can if it's a Bon-Daid. Lucy Ann says ankles are very sexy."

"Lucy Ann? Jane! Anyway, I'm sick of this campaign. All these people I don't even know, know me. The fifth-grade Grimmet stares at me every minute. I can't ever be my real self and bust loose."

"You never bust loose! You're good."

"I feel like busting loose. I can't say even one thing that's stupid. They're listening to every word."

"Say something stupid now," Jane said. "Feel free."

"I can't think of anything. Now."

"That's really stupid," Jane said, "to waste this

gracious opportunity. Bon? It's not that long, anymore. Just next week, and the week after, and the Monday after that is the election."

Bonnie said nothing.

"The rest of us have to be good, too," Jane said. "It's really hard for Jerry and them."

Bonnie didn't answer.

"Hey, and how about the great news about tutoring the second graders in writing: getting them to write to their parents about what a terrific principal you would be. If Mrs. Atkins complains, we say it's 'Practice in Using Adjectives'!"

Bonnie burst out, "I wish we had great news about fifth grade."

"We do! Didn't you hear? The Grimmet got caught kissing Walter Byrnes in the book room."

"Poor Walter!" Bonnie said. "Not gossip, you ninny. Their votes!"

"I don't think he was doing it so she'd vote for you, Bonnie, if that's what you mean. I don't think their minds were on the election."

Bonnie couldn't even laugh. "The worst thing today was, after all that, all the way home Gail bugged me and bugged me about my speech."

She couldn't bear to tell Jane what Gail had actually said. When they reached her home, Gail had run up the steps, then called loudly: "Bonnie, I'll give you this weekend. But I want to see your speech—the whole speech—right after school Monday! I mean it!"

Remembering Gail talking to her like that, remembering that she hadn't answered at all, made Bonnie wince even now. But all she said was, "I'm so sick of Gail."

"It's about time!" Jane said. "Everybody else was sick of her the second day of school. Why don't you stop doing what she says, Bon? I'm used to you being good for teachers, but I can't stand you being good for Gail!"

"I feel like I'm trapped with her in the election, like the third graders in Mrs. Atkins's class. Because . . . she's right about the speech, isn't she?" Bonnie swallowed, afraid she might cry. "Besides, that's not the only thing. I keep thinking, if we win, you all get to be happy. I have to fire Mr. Locke. Jane, I forget it and forget it, then all of a sudden I wake up in the night shivering and sweating about it, worse than Schaffer's nightmares. I forget it in school, then he looks at me and I remember and I want to run out of there."

Bonnie remembered her parents' sad talks after her uncle had been fired a few months before and the long, long telephone calls until finally her father had helped him get a job at another company.

"How can I fire Mr. Locke?" she said. "I know I have to do it, but I know I can't. Do you think I could get the Steering Committee to come with me?"

"Not me!" Jane said. "Mine is the Lists and Planning Committee. We just make the plans. Other people have to do them."

"Thanks a lot," Bonnie said. "Jane. You know what I saw on his desk? Want ads! Like he was looking for a job!"

"Maybe that will save you! He'll just disappear in the night."

"But I told Gail and she said not to count on it. She says he's the kind of teacher who will sit there for the rest of his life saying the same things over and over and over."

"Besides," Jane asked, "who would possibly be ninny enough to give him a job?"

"So I have to fire him. I mean it, Jane. How can I say that to him?"

"I think you just say, 'You're fired,'" Jane said. "Bonnie! Wait! This is it! This is purely beautiful: If you win, *you fire Gail!*"

Then, finally, that good little girl Bonnie Mann laughed a short and very nasty laugh.

11

A Small Glob of Chocolate Pudding

By the next Monday, half the children in D-W were wearing Bon-Daids made from tape the Materials Committee bought with money from the first bake sale and decorated with Gail's multicolor pen. Bonnie secretly thought it was absolutely wonderful to see so many people wearing her sign. She was secretly very sorry when Mrs. Atkins said firmly in her loudspeaker announcements that the only appropriate use of bandages in school was for medical purposes.

That morning, Mr. Locke was at his worst. The homework he had assigned for science had been difficult for almost everyone, but instead of explaining it, he announced a test. When the class cried out, he told them not to interrupt or there would be no recess.

Mrs. Atkins came in at that moment, and he interrupted himself to greet her with a big smile. They stood by the door, whispering loudly, nodding, laughing. As the minutes passed, the class whispered and talked ever more boldly.

Suddenly, Mrs. Atkins turned. "Your sixth graders, Mr. Locke, need to show more responsibility toward their work."

When she was gone, Mr. Locke said angrily. "I expect you to make good use of your time, no matter what I'm doing. Jerry, Michael, you have plenty of work to do."

After the test began, Jane went up to ask him a question. "During a test is too late for questions," he said loudly, cutting her off. "You'll have to pass or fail on what you already know."

At recess, almost the whole class formed an angry, buzzing circle, which grew even angrier when Jane told them that she found Mr. Locke reading the science chapter, himself. "*He* didn't do his homework! That's why we had the test."

As they went in again, to start the math shouts, Jane got Bonnie to try a new game—guessing whom Mr. Locke would pick on first. "His stupid boring rudeness is the same every day," she whispered, "just aimed at a different person."

Neither girl guessed right. Mr. Locke had noticed Schaffer standing just inside the door. "Young man?"

"Can I talk to Bon . . . ?"

"You do not come in here and interrupt a class!" Mr. Locke said.

Schaffer stared for a moment at the teacher, at his sister. He started to open his mouth.

Mr. Locke took a step toward him. "Do you understand?"

Schaffer nodded. "Okay," he whispered, but he didn't move. He seemed frozen by the door.

Mr. Locke took another step. "Do you really understand?" His shoe gave an excruciating screech.

Schaffer gasped and ducked and ran out.

The room was silent for a moment, but when Mr. Locke turned toward his desk and his coffee, many angry voices rose behind him.

"He could at least have asked if it was serious!"

"It's worse when he does it to a little kid!"

"Why worse?"

"He shouldn't be like that to anyone. We just got used to it."

"That guy is a serious ninny!"

Bonnie stood, half ready to go after her brother. Mr. Locke turned. "You will be *quiet*!"

Bonnie sat down.

"Bonnie, you have got to win!" Jane said as most of the Steering Committee walked together on the way to the Big Room for lunch.

"Then we have to get the fifth-grade vote," Bobby said.

"Then we have got to do something about the lunchroom," Bonnie said. "That's the only issue the fifth graders care about."

"King George says she's working on it," Jane said.

"*I'm* working on it," Gail said. "It's driving me crazy. I can't think of a single thing we could do. But I know I'm going to do something. . . ."

A few minutes later, the sixth grade did do something about the lunchroom.

They started a riot.

Actually, the riot may have started because in a meeting of the spelling club just before lunch, Mr. Locke announced that the fifth-grade Grimmet would be the number-one speller for the city-wide meet. The rest of the team would also be fifth graders, except for Lucy Ann, number seven, and Nancy, number nine. As soon as she came into the lunchroom, the Grimmet let everyone know.

Five minutes later, she and Lucy Ann were loudly squabbling over whether a small glob of chocolate pudding had flipped off the lid of one's container onto the nose of the other by accident or on purpose. The question of whose pudding and whose nose was lost to history, for Mr. Locke, who was on duty and whose job it was to report such things, had just stepped over to the teachers' lounge. In any case, the squabble grew.

"Can't we eat a decent meal in peace and quiet around here?" Bonnie yelled.

She was surprised to find herself standing up and yelling, and more surprised to see everyone in the room staring at her, and most surprised to see Nancy also stand, and yell, "Go, Lucy Ann!" and throw both halves of a deviled egg into the face of the fifth-grade Grimmet.

"Get her!" yelled the Grimmet's best friend, and threw a handful of sweet pickle slices at Nancy.

Then, with a roar, the sixth graders rushed in to help Lucy Ann and Nancy with everything in their lunchboxes. The Grimmet's friends rushed in to help her, and the riot was on.

Bonnie ducked some flying hunks of canned peaches and yelled "Go, Lucy Ann!" just because it felt so good. There was no need to yell that, because Lucy Ann, like almost everyone else, was going at full speed.

Pretzels and carrot sticks and other hard foods were simply thrown. Softer foods, like puddings and cottage cheese, were flipped from the ends of plastic spoons.

A very young girl appeared beside Bonnie, clutching her lunchbox. "What should I throw?" she whispered.

Bonnie recognized another good little girl. "Are you scared to throw?"

The little girl nodded.

Bonnie looked into the lunchbox and pulled out a bag. "Why don't you just walk around quietly and crumble potato chips in people's hair? That would help. Could you do that?"

"I think so. Thank you," the little girl whispered and went off to her work.

Bonnie looked into her own lunchbox. She and

Schaffer were particularly lucky: Mrs. Mann had been to a campaign fund-raiser the night before and had brought home coconut puffs, hush puppies, miniature egg rolls, stuffed grape leaves, and radish roses for her children's lunches.

Bonnie tossed a few of these tasty treats this way and that, which was quite pleasant. Then she really wound up and bounced a slightly rancid coconut puff off Gail Dewksbury's head. She felt a shiver of pure happiness as Gail flashed an angry look at the fifth-grade Grimmet's best friend.

"Hey, Bunnie!" the Grimmet called. "You're supposed to be so good!"

"Not today!" Bonnie yelled back and threw a radish rose at the Grimmet. "Bunnie yourself!"

Bonnie felt great, she felt wonderful. She loved the way everyone was working together to make this glorious mess. She watched with admiration as the fifth-grade Grimmet opened her egg salad sandwich, used a celery stick to smear the filling equally on both sides, carried the gooey pieces carefully to where Walter Byrnes was sitting, waited until Walter stood to throw a grape, placed them in the center of his chair, and stood back to watch until Walter Byrnes had sat and he and her egg salad sandwich had risen again.

"Even Gail!" Jane whispered to Bonnie. "This is the best thing we've ever done. Even you! See, Bonnie, see? Have some?" She held out a plastic bag of her lunchtime favorite, shredded cheese mixed with shredded lettuce. They threw handfuls straight up, not at anyone in particular, but making a lovely green and orange rain over all.

Of course, Mr. Locke at last returned. "Excuse me!" he shouted. "Order!"

"It's only Mr. Locke!" someone yelled. Everyone kept throwing.

Mr. Locke grabbed a chair and thumped it against the floor. Three or four children liked the way this added to the racket and did the same.

"Stop this!" Mr. Locke yelled, and grabbed the nearest racing child.

"Owww!" Schaffer, for it was he, spun out of Mr. Locke's mean grip and accidentally slopped hot chicken soup from his thermos into Mr. Locke's shoe.

"Owww!" Mr. Locke yelped, and Bonnie was amazed to see him retreat, racing toward the office for help.

At about this time, the spirit began to go out of the riot, though no one wanted it to be over. The problem was simple: Despite Jerry's good work recovering bits of food from under the tables, people were running out of things to throw.

"This stupid lunchroom!" Gail shouted. Everyone agreed, of course, and watched to see what she would do about it.

"In my old school," she said, "they did it like this!" She poured a little milk onto a napkin and threw the wet paper up with all her strength. When it smacked against the ceiling, there it stayed.

"Okay!" All eyes shifted to Bobby Roberts as he poured milk onto his napkin. The room was silent. But when Bobby Roberts's napkin also stuck to the ceiling, Lucy Ann yelled "Whoopee!" and pandemonium broke out.

Luckily almost no one had yet used a napkin. Soon, thirty, forty napkins slowly dripped milk from the Big Room ceiling.

But almost immediately there was a shortage of napkins. Again, Gail came to the rescue: "Paper towels!" she yelled. Two girls, two boys, headed down the hall in opposite directions.

Bonnie stood by the door, ready to help pass out the towels. For the first time, she began to notice the slimy feeling of pudding-in-the-ear, the squishy feeling of warm-milk-in-the-shoe, the scratchy feeling of pretzels-down-the-back.

When the door opened again, it revealed not messengers returning with supplies, but Mrs. Atkins, looking grim, with Mr. Locke, Mrs. Tilley, Miss Everts, and Miss Camp all looking grim behind her.

Instantly, the room was still. No one moved. No one spoke.

After looking around the room, glancing for a fraction of a second into every single face, Mrs. Atkins folded her arms across her belt and began to speak. As she was getting to the heart of her message ("Misbehavior in the lunchroom is as inappropriate as misbehavior in the class"), one napkin, heavy with milk, slowly worked itself loose from the ceiling above her and fell with a loud, wet *Smack!* onto her right shoulder.

Bonnie didn't breathe. She heard a slight snort and saw Mrs. Tilley, her hand over her mouth, back quickly into the hall.

Mrs. Atkins stopped speaking. She removed the soggy napkin and with a graceful gesture held it at arm's length to her side. She pressed her lips together and again looked around the room.

Bonnie wondered if every other kid felt, as she did, that that had been *her* napkin. She wondered if every other kid was also trying not to laugh.

After a moment, Mrs. Atkins continued: "Everyone will pick up his or her lunchbox and thermos and return to his or her own classroom. There will be no recess today. The sixth grade will stay, Mr. Locke, and under your supervision restore this room to its proper order. Although they have been working for weeks on a very mature project, the sixth graders were obviously unable to control themselves today, unable to provide an example of good citizenship for the younger children. We expect our sixth graders to be more mature."

Gail murmured, "Not fair!"

Mrs. Atkins frowned. "We shall have to decide whether the sixth graders are mature enough to continue with their project." She turned to Bonnie. "Please put this where it belongs."

Bonnie looked at the wastebasket right by Mrs. Atkins's feet. She could feel the muscles in her arm, as if she were pulling a great weight, trying *not* to do what Mrs. Atkins wanted. She could feel her mouth trying to say that the fifth graders were just as guilty.

But Mrs. Atkins continued to stare at her, and Bonnie looked away. She could take part in the riot; she could not defy Mrs. Atkins in front of everyone. She took the soggy napkin and dropped it into the trash.

As the children began to leave, the fifth-grade Grimmet smiled up at Mrs. Atkins. "Mrs. Atkins, they . . ."

"Later, dear," Mrs. Atkins said.

Bonnie felt pressure on her back.

"Good-bye, Bunnie." The fifth-grade Grimmet smiled.

A moment later, Jane told Bonnie there was a large, almost perfect, chocolate pudding handprint on the back of her blouse.

The sixth graders spent the next two hours using Mr. Lipchik's equipment to scrub the tables, benches, floor, walls, and ceiling of the Big Room, and to scrub themselves.

Far from being ashamed, and still much too excited to take notice of Mrs. Atkins's threat, Bonnie simply enjoyed the rest of the afternoon. Gossiping and giggling, whispering about King George, and remembering the best parts were almost as good as the riot itself. Like the others, Bonnie took great pride in the extraordinary mess. In a way, Mrs. Atkins had been right: It *had* been the sixth grade's riot, because they had cooperated so wonderfully, rushing to help Lucy Ann.

Only Gail was unhappy. "Bonnie, that was terrible," she said, interrupting Jane's giggling whisper. "I can't believe I didn't try to stop it."

Jane made a face at Bonnie that she didn't even bother to hide from Gail.

Gail paid no attention. "We have to think of something fast if we're going to save the project. Let's have a meeting right after . . ."

"No!" Jane said. "No meeting! Forget it for once, will you, Gail? See you tomorrow. See you next week."

Gail gave Jane a look. "Wait for me after school, Bonnie," she said, and left.

The most interesting moment of her afternoon, though, was when Bonnie found herself carrying trash bags outside with Bobby Roberts. She couldn't think of anything to say and neither, it seemed, could he. They walked out, dumped their bags, and were starting back when Bobby asked, "Well, how did you enjoy the riot?"

"Yes!" Bonnie said, in a voice somewhere between a whisper and a squeak.

Bobby nodded. "That was really good."

Bonnie shook her head. "That was really bad!" The way Bobby laughed made her wonder if he had the same problem she did. "Do people tease you for being good?" she asked shyly.

"Oh, yeah," he said. "Walter, especially. That's why today was so great."

"Me, too," Bonnie said. "Today, the good guys were really bad!"

"It was the right thing to do," Bobby said.

She smiled, and they both nodded, and for a little while longer Bonnie didn't care what the results of the riot might be.

But there was no way she could avoid listening to Gail worry all the way home. Gail had no idea what to do to save the election project. Bonnie had never heard her sound so uncertain.

As they reached Gail's steps, Bonnie tried to get back to the fun of it. "I didn't know you could go so crazy!"

"I didn't know you could be so bad," Gail said, quietly. "Our only hope is if King George doesn't want to make a big deal about so many kids going wild, right before the election."

Now I'm in trouble for being bad! Bonnie thought indignantly. But she knew this had not been the kind of bad that accomplished good, not the kind Mr. Lipchik had once recommended.

12

The Closest to a Boy/Girl Party

For the rest of the week, the whole sixth grade tried to be good, tried not to call attention to the election project. Gail canceled a Steering Committee meeting. Jerry canceled the next bake sale. Lucy Ann canceled tutoring second graders. Gail didn't even ask to see Bonnie's speech. Jane and Shawna and Nancy and Gillian went around with their fingers crossed.

Then at Friday assembly, after announcing that a parent as well as a teacher would be on lunchroom duty each day, Mrs. Atkins spoke at length about the need to be good citizens and the need to be mature. But she announced no specific punishment, and Bonnie knew the election project was safe.

Back in the classroom, Jane grumbled loudly: "Matoor! Matoor! I hate the word 'matoor.' If I have to grow backward to a baby, I'm never going to be boring, boring, boring matoor!"

For the first time since the riot, the sixth graders laughed together.

*   *   *

For Bonnie and Jerry, the happiness didn't last long. Skipping off to announce that there *would* be another bake sale, they hadn't even started down the stairs when Mrs. Atkins's firm voice stopped them short, as if they were frolicking dogs who suddenly hit the end of their leash.

"Excuse me! May I ask where you are going? You know two children are not allowed out of a classroom at the same time."

Bonnie and Jerry quickly explained their errand *and* that they had Mr. Locke's permission.

"Well." Mrs. Atkins stared at them until they looked away.

"The bake sale . . ." Jerry said. "We have to . . ."

"What you *have* to do is schoolwork. You have a great deal of work to do, Jerry, before you will be ready to pass to junior high."

"Mrs. Atkins," Bonnie said, "this *is* schoolwork. The bake sales are part of the election project, for American history."

"Your father tells me, Bonnie, that you also have a great deal to do, especially in math. There will be no more bake sales."

"*Why?*"

"You needn't ask 'why,' Bonnie," Mrs. Atkins said cooly. "You also have a great deal to learn, it seems, about respecting those who are older and wiser. It is up to your teacher, with guidance from his principal, if necessary, to decide what is, and what is not, educational. It is up to us to be sure that the election project does not get out of hand, that it does not take more than its appropriate place in the curriculum and the school day. I will meet with Mr. Locke this afternoon. In any case, I assure you, there will be no more bake sales. You may return to your classroom."

"Do you think she knows we mean it?" Jerry whispered to Bonnie just before they went in. "Is she scared you'll beat her?"

"I don't think so. I don't think she could believe kids could do such a thing. She just likes working her power. I think."

That afternoon, the weather turned cold and wet. As other children hurried home, the Steering Committee members huddled by the high rock, trying to find shelter from the bitter wind.

"Let's not have a meeting," Lucy Ann said. "Meetings are as bad as school."

"Yes!" Gail said. "This one will be different. It has to be. The election is a week from Monday, and we just lost a week's work and got ourselves a bad reputation."

"Let's go to my house," Bonnie said, stamping her feet. "At least we'll be warm."

"Won't your mom hear what we're talking about?" Jane whispered to Bonnie as, half running against the wind, they led the way. "Won't she think it's weird you brought boys?"

"She won't notice. Her mind is on the campaign. Her campaign."

When she heard the group come in, Mrs. Mann ran up from the basement, her arms full of envelopes.

"Hi, Mom," Bonnie said. "May we have a meeting here?"

"Hi, kids! Of course, Bon. I think there're English muffins in the freezer. And some pickles. I have *got* to go to the store! Would you all mind hauling some of these to the mailbox when you leave, Jane? Jerry? We're getting out a last-minute mailing. Oh, and your dad's pasta sauce; that might taste great on the muffins."

"Thanks, Mom," Bonnie said. "I'll take care of it."

Mrs. Mann went back down to the basement.

"There's always cinnamon," Bonnie said to Jerry after they had opened and closed this and that, trying to find something good. The others were looking over the campaign materials stacked on the dining-room table. Bonnie heated up apple juice with cinnamon in it, and Jerry sprinkled the toasted English muffins with cinnamon sugar.

As she carried in the tray, Bonnie was struck by the chaos in the Manns' living room caused by only six sixth graders—and their jackets, umbrellas, and mittens, notebooks, textbooks, sneakers and boots, lunchboxes, Jerry's soccer ball, and Lucy Ann's large roll of posters. She understood completely why some parents might not want a class party in their home.

"So," Lucy Ann asked, "did anyone get an idea for our slogan?"

"How about 'Bonnie! Bonnie! She's our Mann!'?" asked Jerry.

"I am not!" Bonnie said.

"Okay, okay," Gail said. "Let's talk about the fifth. Jerry, what about those guys you play ball with?"

"The problem is," Jerry said, "they pretty well like D-W. I told them they won't be so happy next year, when they have Locke."

"But they *like* him," Jane said. "They think Mrs. Tilley is a little kooky!"

"Mrs. Tilley makes them think, you know," Lucy Ann said. "They hate that. It's a strain on their little brains."

"I give up on them!" Jane said.

"We can't give up on them!" Bonnie said.

"The trouble is, they think Daniel Webster"— Jerry sighed and the whole committee was able to finish—"is a good little school!"

At that moment, Mrs. Mann rushed into the room, a scrap of paper in her hand. She smiled at their words and said, "I'm sorry to interrupt you people, but maybe you can help me."

"Sure, Mrs. Mann," Jane said, as they all closed their notebooks over their lists and charts and poster sketches.

"Bonnie's dad just called. You know he works for Complex—they're developing an experiment package for the next moon landing. One of the astronauts is coming to his office Monday." She waited while everyone murmured excitedly. "The experiment requires the astronaut to bend over, and the big question is whether his space suit will let him bend far enough. He's coming to bend for them." She laughed. "The work that goes into being a hero!

"Anyway, this fellow's flying in Monday for a nine-o'clock meeting. The astronaut office asked if there was anywhere he could speak at eight. They like to slip in a little public relations. I wish he would speak for my candidate. . . ."

Gail started to say something, but Mrs. Mann went rushing on.

"But the astronauts can't do anything political. Boss Tweed once said the art of politics is being ready to take advantage of anything that happens. 'Readiness is all,' he said. But I'm darned if I see how to take advantage of this."

"Would he speak at school?" Gail asked. "Like at an assembly?"

Bonnie was so astonished at her mother's quotation, wondering what this readiness stuff was all about and who was Boss Tweed, anyway? that she didn't notice at first what Gail was up to.

"That's just the kind of thing," Mrs. Mann said. "But the children aren't there by eight. How could we get the word out? We could do a marathon tele-phoning, I suppose, if anyone had time."

Gail stood up slowly, talking all the while. "Mrs. Mann, if you call Mrs. Atkins to arrange it, we'll organize our class to phone the whole school. If she'd give us the class lists with all the phone numbers, it would be easy. We don't have much homework this weekend."

"No," Jane said. "No! We can do it!"

As Mrs. Mann left to call Mrs. Atkins, Gail and Jane made quick plans to copy the class lists.

"Great!" Bobby said. "Now we'll know exactly how many kids and how many parents."

"We'll know where the little kids live, so we can offer to bring them to the meeting to vote, even if their parents don't come," Jane said.

"This assembly is just what we need," Gail said. "They'll forget all about the riot, if we do it right."

Bonnie was bothered. She didn't like the way Gail was acting sneaky toward her dear, trusting, dis-tracted mother. Gail wasn't lying, exactly, and everyone else was excited, but Bonnie didn't like it at all.

"An astronaut!" Jerry said. "Now those fifth grad-ers will see what we can do!"

"When people phone the kids," Gail said, "it's important to mention that it's Bonnie Mann's father who's arranging it, Bonnie Mann in sixth, and end up saying 'Bonnie Mann hopes you can come.' "

"No!" When the others turned at the sharpness in Bonnie's voice, she smiled. "Mom just said the astronauts aren't supposed to do politics. Anyway, it isn't me that's doing it. It has nothing to do with me."

"Anyway, Gail, that's too phony!" Jane said. "I'd be gagging on giggles."

Gail stared at Bonnie. "Okay. Okay, but then at least Bonnie better call every fifth grader herself."

Bonnie made a face, but she felt she had to agree.

"Call me, Bon," Jane said, "whenever you can't stand them anymore."

"Gail," Jerry said, "I hate to tell you, but that's not going to work, about getting the rest of them to help call. My committee . . ." That afternoon, Mr. Locke had caught the Budget and Fund-Raising Committee playing poker in the boys' room using money borrowed from the bake sale fund. "Those guys aren't interested anymore."

"My committee's bored, too," Lucy Ann said. "Gail? They'd work if they knew we're really trying to win, to get rid of Mr. Locke."

"No. We can't tell anybody else yet," Gail said. "We can't risk having the grown-ups find out. The election's on a Monday night. We won't tell the rest of the class till that morning. But most of the kids would probably phone, Jerry, for an astronaut."

"Mrs. Mann!" Bobby said loudly as she came back

into the room. "Which one is it? Which astronaut?"

"I hope it's PB&J!" Jerry said.

"What does that mean, Jerry?" Mrs. Mann asked. "I don't follow all that technical NASA jargon."

"Well . . . peanut butter and jelly," Jerry said. "See, he snuck this sandwich up because he was tired of eating mush out of tubes."

"Okay, if even a crumb got loose in zero gravity," Bobby said, "it could gum up the works. NASA didn't like it."

"I loved it," said Jerry. "I was eating one exactly when they announced it. PB&J is the greatest!"

Mrs. Mann looked at her note. "Mr. Mann didn't say who it was. Anyway, Mrs. Atkins had left school, but Miss Boyard was sure she would agree. If you go over now, she'll have the class lists for you."

Jane and Gail left immediately. At the front door, Jane whispered to Bonnie: "Keep them here. We'll run. Keep them here! This is probably the closest I'm ever going to get in my entire pathetic childhood to a boy/girl party."

Astonished that such an event might be occurring in her own home, Bonnie tiptoed back into the living room. Sure enough, Bobby and Jerry and Lucy Ann were fooling around about slogan ideas and football scores and what's the best trimmings on pizza, and soon Bonnie was talking and laughing, too. She was amazed to learn that Bobby Roberts also liked pepperoni and double cheese pizza best. It seemed no time before Gail and Jane were back with the lists, and with potato chips and sodas.

"We stopped at Gail's on the way back," Jane told Bonnie in the kitchen as they unpacked the food. "Her mom is nice! She gave us all this stuff. Hey, Bon. Gail arranged with Miss Boyard for you to introduce the astronaut."

Bonnie felt sheer terror. "To the assembly?"

"Where else? Well, you could introduce him to Miss Boyard. She is in a twit! You know how she stays home for every launch and splashdown? She's already arranged for Mr. Lipchik to open school early. She's planning to wear her sky-blue dress and a pin her friend brought her from the launch of Gemini Five; she has her hair appointment; and she's going to bring a pitcher and a glass from home, in case he gets thirsty."

"Gail had no right to do that without asking me!" Bonnie was pouring the soda so furiously, one glass after another overflowed.

"I told you and told you about her, Bon. But look what her mother gave us, three kinds of chips!"

"She's trying to make everyone think the astronaut is on our side. She has no right! I told her just now! . . ."

"But you were so polite, Bon. You'll never get her to do anything, being so polite. You're going to have to yell at her. Don't you ever fight with Schaffer?" Jane asked kindly. "Do you need me to teach you some words?"

"I *know* the words. I just don't . . . Jane, how can I get up in front of all those people?"

"You can do it! It's good practice for your speech election night, so you won't be nervous then."

"What about nervous now? What about nervous twice? Miss Cherry never gave speeches," Bonnie pointed out. "Miss Cherry hid in her office and used the loudspeaker. What can I say?"

"Say something great about the great space program and the great astronauts," Jane said, her mouth full of potato chips. "It's not such a big deal, Bonnie. If a man can go to the moon, you can introduce an astronaut."

"I'm sick of hearing that for an excuse for everything," Bonnie said, as she followed Jane in to the unexpected party. "Some things are hard." At least, with the astronaut assembly to organize, Gail seemed to have forgotten about the election night speech.

13

Being Polite to Gail

The astronaut politely shook hands with Bonnie and Schaffer, then he and Mr. Mann talked business all the way to school.

Mr. Mann parked in the No Parking space right in front. Mrs. Atkins hurried over, shaking her head, her lips tight, but as the car was quickly surrounded by a noisy crowd of children and quite a few parents, she soon was smiling graciously. Bonnie and Schaffer ran to join their friends.

The astronaut looked terrific: He stood tall and straight, he grinned, he waved to the crowd. He shook hand with Mrs. Atkins and with Mr. Grimmet, the PAT president, who had suddenly included himself in the proceedings.

"I didn't exactly think he'd have on his space stuff," Jane said, "but why did he have to wear a suit and tie?"

"And a briefcase!" Nancy said. "He looks like some old dad."

Bonnie, feeling stiff with fright, walked between

them as they joined the crowd going into the building. She had reduced her introduction to a single sentence, but there was no way to make it shorter than that.

"Jerry!" Jane said. "Why are you wearing a Bon-Daid? You're going to get us in trouble with Mrs. Atkins all over again."

Jerry looked proudly at the gorgeous red, white, and blue double strip Bon-Daid smack in the middle of his navy blue shirt. "Gail told me to. She called me last night and told me to get my whole committee to wear them. She says Mrs. Atkins will be too busy to notice. It's just a little reminder for everybody about Bonnie." He gave Bonnie such a warm smile her heart sank.

"She doesn't give up, does she?" Jane said.

"Jerry, take it off. Please?" Bonnie said.

Jerry looked confused. "We're going to spread out all over the hall."

"Please, Jerry, please? And tell your friends, too." When he left, Bonnie told Jane, "She called me, last night, too. She wanted me to say, 'The astronaut is brought to you by the sixth-grade election project,' like an ad or something."

"Are you going to?"

"No! I told her it was my family's astronaut, and I would never insult him that way."

"Good for you, Bon! Did you yell, or were you just polite?"

"Well, I was polite," Bonnie said. "But it's my introduction, and she can't make me say anything I don't want to."

"What did she say?"

"She didn't say anything. She just said, 'Well,' you know, like Mrs. Atkins does."

"You'd better watch out, then. Gail does what she wants, no matter what." Bonnie made a face and headed off toward the front of the hall. "Good luck with your speech!" Jane called after her.

Because Daniel Webster was a small school with no auditorium, assemblies were held in the second-floor hall. This morning, Mr. Lipchik had placed a few chairs at one end, facing the audience, and a tall wooden podium where the speaker could rest his papers. Here, Miss Boyard had placed her pretty little pitcher and her glass. Mr. Grimmet seemed about to take Bonnie's chair at the end of the little row in front, but Miss Boyard firmly told him he would have to find another.

Bonnie didn't notice the fuss; she didn't notice Mr. Lipchik watching her as he adjusted the podium lamp. She looked out over the crowded hall, terrified.

"Good morning, teachers and children of Daniel Webster School," Mrs. Atkins began. "We are happy so many parents were able to attend this very special occasion. We are extremely honored to have with us today a truly genuine American hero, a man who has flown to the moon and back. I understand that Bonnie Mann is going to formally welcome him to our school."

Mrs. Atkins turned to find Mr. Grimmet right behind her, winking and grinning. Redheaded, blue-eyed Mr. Grimmet looked exactly like the Grimmet children, except for a little gray in his hair, and a few wrinkles at the edges of his eyes.

"Just a moment, Mrs. Atkins, Bonnie," he said. "I just want to say a word on behalf of the parents, administrators, and teachers, just to say how gratified we are at the honor you do us, Mr. . . . Capt . . ." He grinned the Grimmet grin out over the audience.

"A pathetic sight! A grown man trying to look adorable!"

Startled, Bonnie soon discovered Mr. Lipchik adjusting an electrical connection right behind her chair, and soon, like an out-of-season mosquito, he was buzzing again in her ear: "I do believe the poor man is trying very hard not to say, 'Captain Peanut Butter and Jelly.' "

This time a laugh sputtered through Bonnie's tight lips.

"Don't worry about your speech," Mr. Lipchik said. "That podium will hide all but the top of your head."

"Thank you!" Bonnie whispered as Mr. Grimmet finished awkwardly: ". . . as a representative of the space program."

Bonnie was up and speaking and sitting down again in ten seconds. "Daniel Webster Elementary School is proud to welcome the great astronaut, the great Joe Rattling!"

The crowd went wild, and Mr. Lipchik was able to speak right out loud: "That may be the single most effective campaign speech, word for word, ever delivered in the history of our great republic."

"It was easy," Bonnie said. "I knew his name."

"Now you're finished, I'll go," he said, putting the pliers in his pocket and taking a dead cigar off his ear. "I have better things to do than listen to one of these fellows."

"Good-bye," Bonnie whispered, as the applause died down. "Thanks."

Joe Rattling set his watch on the podium. "Good morning. Thank you. I'm not going to make a speech at you, and I'll tell you why.

"By the time you get to be an astronaut, you've gone to elementary school, junior high, senior high, college, taken a couple of graduate degrees, post-doctoral work, flight training, maybe test pilot school. Most of us have also been in the military. Then, you find your education has only begun. Now you study astronomy, geology, physics, aero-dynamics, navigation, computers, basic medicine. You also have to learn how to fly your particular spacecraft for your particular mission.

"So if I start at 0800 hours today spilling out everything that's been poured into my head, I might not be finished talking by the time you're old enough to start astronaut training yourselves."

There was a ripple of pleased laughter at that.

"Also, I might not tell you what you want to know," Joe Rattling said. "So, please ask me some questions."

After the briefest pause for shyness, the questions came fast:

"What does a blast-off feel like?"

"What takes longer, going to the moon or coming back?"

"How do you swallow food when you're upside down in no gravity?"

"What's it like, bouncing on the moon?"

This last question, Joe Rattling couldn't answer. Although he had traveled *to* the moon, he had not actually landed *on* the moon. He had been the third astronaut on his crew, who stayed in the Command Module orbiting the moon, while the other two landed on the surface.

He seemed to sense the children's disappointment. "It was my assignment, as simple as that," he said. "I felt lucky to be on the mission at all."

"How long were you alone in the CM?" someone asked.

"About a day and a half." He looked behind him. "Yes, Bonnie?"

"Weren't you lonely?" His trip had reminded her of the week her family had gone to the shore, but she got strep throat and had to stay on the beach while the others swam.

He shrugged. "I was prepared for it. There was usually someone from Mission Control on the radio, giving me figures for my computer or telling me the football scores. Mostly you're so busy, you don't have a chance to be lonely."

The astronaut poured water from the pitcher and took a sip from the glass. Miss Boyard sighed so loudly, Bonnie wondered if she had been holding her breath until that moment.

"I'll tell you when I did feel lonely, Bonnie: when the CM passed behind the moon. When you're over the far side of the moon, you can't see Earth and you can't speak with Earth—the radio waves don't curve around to reach you. When you're alone in the CM behind the moon, for forty-eight long minutes you're about as alone as a human being can be."

"Weren't you scared then?" Bonnie asked. "If something went wrong, and you couldn't even tell them . . ."

"Any test pilot will tell you it's dangerous, trying a vehicle that new. But we're trained. We're ready to handle almost anything. A fine astronaut, Mike Collins, summed it up best: 'Readiness is all.' "

Behind him, Bonnie grinned.

Joe Rattling picked up his watch. "I have to be taking off now. . . ."

A kindergarten child gasped.

"No, not literally," Joe Rattling said. "In Mr. Mann's station wagon. Well, I've enjoyed it. Thank you for inviting me."

He waved to the cheering crowd, which was already racing out to watch the great Joe Rattling leave. The playground was soon a universe of spaceships blasting off in all directions, a carnival bumper car ride with every car out of control, a beehive with the bees gone mad.

"How come you talked so much?" Jane asked Bonnie when the bell finally rang and they moved inside again. "I thought you were so scared."

Bonnie blushed. "I guess I forgot. He was so amazing. He was so brave."

"Bonnie!"

The shout was loud and commanding, and many other children stopped and turned as Bonnie did.

It was Gail Dewksbury, standing on the landing halfway between the first and second floors, leaning over the rail, waving both arms.

When almost everyone was looking at her, she shouted again, "Bonnie! Thank you!" She leaned farther out over the crowd. "That was wonderful! Thank you, Bonnie!"

For just a second, Bonnie didn't know what Gail was talking about. Then the children began to crowd around her, kindergarteners to fifth graders, straining and stretching to look at her, repeating what Gail had said, and more. "Hey, yeah!" "Thanks, Bonnie!" "That was great!" "Do you know him?"

"That was the best thing I ever saw!" "Thank you, Bonnie!"

Bonnie was startled by the many voices, embarrassed by the many eyes.

The children surged around her, pressing close, as if she were the astronaut herself, as if another riot were about to start, around her. The third-grade Grimmet asked her for her autograph, and then six, ten more children asked.

Bonnie looked up, furious, and saw Gail grinning back down.

With her friends' help, Bonnie pushed her way through the crowd to the stairs; then she raced up, leaving the shouting children behind, leaving her friends, stomping quickly by Gail as well, without a look, without a word, racing to the girls' room.

Burning mad at Gail for turning the great Joe Rattling's great visit into just another piece of the campaign, she splashed her face with cold water. Jane was right. She was going to have to stop being polite. She promised herself that somehow, someday—maybe after the election—she would find the courage to yell at Gail.

14

A Fierce and
Useful Temper

The next day, sick of the campaign, angry at Gail, angrier at herself for not fighting back, Bonnie stayed home.

She had no trouble persuading her parents. That's one good thing about being good, she thought. They know I must have some good reason.

She walked around the house with her bathrobe buttoned crooked and her hair not brushed. She said dumb things back to the television set and ate disgusting food, and she thought happily, No one knows.

About three thirty, for her after-school snack, she put thin slices of cheddar cheese on thin crackers, mashed a leftover boiled onion on each one, gave them a sprinkling of chili powder, then put them under the broiler for a minute. She made two glasses of chocolate milk with cinnamon and took the snack and her book to the back room and stretched out along a slant of sunlight on the fuzzy brown rug.

The phone rang.

Lucy Ann, then Jane, then Nancy called. Bonnie cut each call short, only to have the phone ring again almost instantly. The big news of the day was that the class had decorated the room with campaign posters.

None of it sounded important to Bonnie. I stayed home to be safe from it for one day, she thought, and now! . . . That campaign is not worth it. Or I guess it would be, if I only knew . . . She realized there was one person she *did* want to talk with.

She was dressed and running out the door, just as Schaffer came up the steps.

"You're not sick," he said.

"I wish I got to stay home!" he called.

"I'm not voting for you anyway!" he shouted.

By then Bonnie was far up the sidewalk.

There were few children left outside school. Bonnie went to the rear door, which was right by the basement stairs, but also dangerously close to the office.

Cracking the door open, she heard Mrs. Atkins explaining something slowly and precisely. There was no one in sight. In a few seconds, Bonnie was racing down the stairs and through the basement door.

The school basement, with its low ceilings and no windows, consisted of a furnace room, a workshop, several large rooms storing furniture, and the small room Mr. Lipchik had made his own.

There, he had the old stuffed chair Bonnie remembered with a standing lamp tilting over it, a little shelf for his books, and a table made of four upside-down plastic milk crates where he put his lunch, his ashtray, and the wooden radio he had found in Bonnie's alley. On the wall opposite, he had hung two bright paintings from the art room. A huge heating pipe passed near his chair, and in cold weather Mr. Lipchik swung around to keep his feet and his coffee mug warm on that. That was how Bonnie had seen him many times, and that was how she found him now, smoking his cigar and reading.

"Afternoon." Mr. Lipchik looked up and smiled. "I noticed you played hooky. You're getting down-right wicked."

Bonnie made a face. "I wanted to ask you . . ." She warmed her hands on the heating pipe.

Mr. Lipchik closed the big atlas he had been studying, turned the radio down a little, and sat smoking.

Bonnie sat on one of the crates. She heard a huge boiler hissing and the *tick-tick-tick* of metal joints expanding.

This was the first time, she realized, that she had come to Mr. Lipchik. Before, he had just appeared, offering her help or ideas when she didn't even know she needed them. She remembered the magical night before school began when he had come slowly down the alley, reading by the light of the moon.

She put her hands on her knees and leaned forward. "What I need to know is: Are we going to win?"

Mr. Lipchik frowned, and Bonnie rushed on: "I thought, because you know history, and . . . and you're kind of different. . . ." She hoped that wasn't insulting. "Maybe you could tell . . . ?"

"Different isn't magic," Mr. Lipchik said. "It's just different. I give myself the peace and quiet, and the time, to think—*that* may be why I know some things. But I have no idea what will happen. Why did you want to know?"

"This stupid campaign would be worth it, if . . ." Bonnie said. "It would be easier to be brave—like Lincoln, or somebody, winning the war—if I only knew."

"Mr. Lincoln didn't know. He had no idea he'd get out of it with his scalp on and all those compliments in the history books. He had a terrible lonely time of it, at first. He was losing that war. For years! He couldn't even get his own generals to do what he wanted. He fired generals right and left before he put his money on Ulysses S. Grant. . . ."

"Abraham Lincoln? Fired generals?"

"Mr. Lincoln fired generals by the trashcanful. He had to. They weren't doing their job."

Bonnie nodded, and nodded, and grinned a very small grin.

"Even Grant, though he is my own personal hero, was no sure bet. He was a boozer. He was a failure in business, like so many good people. General Grant put things right for Mr. Lincoln, eventually, but Lincoln had no idea beforehand. Oh, no! That's what took the courage, and the patience: keeping on when he didn't know."

Bonnie felt she had just had a scolding. "Mr. Lipchik, there's some ways you aren't fair," she said. "Remember you told me General Grant said, 'Readiness is all'?"

He nodded. "A wise man."

"Well, whoever said it was a grown-up and already tired. Anyway, it sounds like 'Get all ready, then just sit and wait for somebody else to start things, for somebody else to tell you what to do.' Sit and wait like waiting for a bus. Grown-ups just like to show they have the power!"

Mr. Lipchik looked mildly surprised. "Have I joined the villains?" Then he heard something Bonnie did not and went into the furnace room.

Though she was pleased to have discovered a fierce and useful temper in herself, Bonnie knew it wasn't hard—and it was rather foolish—to fight her friend Mr. Lipchik. It wasn't much harder than throwing a coconut puff at Gail when she wasn't looking. But maybe it's practice, she thought, for really fighting Gail. Watching a little cloud of cigar smoke rise and bounce against the ceiling, she tried to get her anger under control.

"You know," Mr. Lipchik said as he came back in and sat down, "if that woman is elected, she's liable to get herself appointed permanent principal here. I'd just have to pack my things and move!"

He raised an eyebrow and looked unhappily at Bonnie. "Perhaps you didn't realize what a difficult business politics is. It's probably too much for a good little girl like . . ."

"Not anymore!" The words burst out of her.

"Now, I didn't intend to insult . . ."

"That 'readiness' idea is like what Mrs. Atkins wants. Just sit there, and listen to them, and be cooperative, no matter what. Gail was right: 'Good' means we don't act up, that's all good means to them." She took a deep breath. "And if you even noticed, I'm not so good, anymore. I'm running for principal!"

Mr. Lipchik tried to say something, but Bonnie couldn't stop:

"Anyway, what's so bad if I *am* good? That's the way I am. I have a right! I just wish everyone would stop noticing it. The only bad part would be if I *didn't* do anything." Bonnie opened the door sharply, ready to run out. "Why shouldn't somebody good start something, once in a while?"

"Careful!" Mr. Lipchik said, leaping up. "The meeting's running late, and once she lets them loose, they stampede out of here."

Bonnie heard a door open, and footsteps and voices. She heard Mrs. Tilley and Mr. Locke teasing loudly about which team would make the Super Bowl. She heard Mrs. Atkins telling Miss Boyard exactly what she wanted on her desk the next morning.

Five minutes later, the building was silent. Bonnie ran up the steps, and Mr. Lipchik opened the heavy door for her.

"I know it's hard," he said. "I mean to do everything I can to help you win."

"I know," said Bonnie. "Thank you, Mr. Lipchik."

Once she was walking along the empty sidewalks under the empty boughs of the willow oaks, Bonnie realized that talking with Mr. Lipchik had helped her a great deal. She had stood up for herself in a way she never had before. She felt so strong and purposeful, she was certain if she was elected, she could make Daniel Webster a better school. She had also found out she was determined to win.

15

On the Far Side
of the Moon

"Bonnie?"

"Yes," she said. "What can I do for you?" She was not surprised, the next morning, when the first person she met was the kindergarden Grimmet. There wasn't much time before the vote next Monday for him to perfect his bargain. She could almost guess what it was.

"Bonnie? If you was the principal?"

"You should say: If you *were* the principal." Bonnie smiled into the cute little boy's cute and sneaky little eyes.

"If you *were* the principal, and we get two guineas and two rabbits, and they have babies, can we keep the babies?"

"Sure," said the candidate. What did a few more beasts in the kindergarten matter?

"All the babies? The second time and the third time and the babies' babies?"

Bonnie vividly remembered the stink from a classroom with too many rodents, a stink that had seeped into the hall every time the door opened, and the teacher's shriek: "Don't touch that guinea pig!"

"No," she said. "You may keep the first two baby rabbits and the first two baby guinea pigs. The rest you have to give away."

"But you learn more if you keep them all! Every kid could have . . ."

"All the babies after that you have to sell, to get the money to buy the pellets to feed the ones you keep." The Grimmet stared at her, and she stared back. "When I am the principal."

The kindergarten Grimmet walked away, kicking at pebbles.

Bonnie skipped across the playground, kicking a few pebbles herself. She found her friends happy and excited, talking about plans for the Sitting Station they were setting up in Bobby Roberts's basement. She stood at the edge of the group, laughing at nothing much.

Gail and Bobby started going over vote totals. "The astronaut didn't help much with fifth," Gail said. "But fourth is all for us. It looks good. We're going to get a lot of kids there."

Bonnie thought the truth was no one knew how anyone would vote, once they found out the election project was real. She barely listened to the vote analyses, anymore; she just kept an ear out so she could enjoy it whenever Bobby Roberts mentioned her name.

"Okay. We got kids in different classes to ask at home," he said. "Not many parents are going to bother coming. They're sure Mrs. Atkins will take care of things. None of them seem to even notice that Bonnie is running."

Bonnie was surprised they had been able to keep the secret this long, that almost everyone still thought the project was just a classroom Experience in Democracy. Only the Steering Committee knew how serious their effort really was and how well it was going. Or perhaps, Bonnie thought, only Gail knew. Sometimes she felt everything was happening according to a secret plan that only Gail controlled.

She moved away now, hoping Gail wouldn't ask about her speech. She and Gail hadn't spoken since the astronaut assembly, and that was fine with Bonnie; she had a low-burning anger at Gail, and low-burning guilt herself, for she still hadn't written more than a few stupid-sounding sentences. If things were going as well as Gail said, maybe her speech wouldn't be so important after all.

That afternoon when the class came back after lunch, they found Mr. Locke standing by his desk, watching the clock.

"I have a very exciting announcement," he began, right at one. "It seems we are going to have a real election."

The class buzzed. Bonnie and Jane glanced sideways at each other.

"I've spoken with Mrs. Atkins," Mr. Locke went on, "about whether we should continue with the Experiment in Democracy, now that there is a third candidate. . . ."

A third candidate! Bonnie was outraged; she felt attacked, as if someone had butted into *her* own private election. The buzz grew louder around her.

"Quiet!" Mr. Locke yelled, then continued. "Mrs. Atkins agreed that since we've already announced it to the parents, and since it will make no difference in the results, we should go ahead. If the sixth graders can be well-behaved at the . . ."

Jane had her hand in the air.

"Jane?"

"I move we continue the election project. We shouldn't give up."

"It's hardly a question of giving up," Mr. Locke said, "in a classroom exercise. Rather, it's a question of complete self-control"—he looked around the room slowly—"at the PAT meeting."

"I second the motion," Lucy Ann said.

"All in favor say 'Aye,' " Mr. Locke said.

"Aye!" boomed the class.

"Well, then," Mr. Locke said sternly. "I will expect you to spend the next few days in a scholarly manner. Bobby, your committee will have to research elections where there were three candidates."

"More parents will come now," Bobby said.

"But their vote will split," Walter pointed out. "Between Mrs. Atkins and . . ."

There was a roar of whispers across the room.

"Mr. Locke?" Gail said. "You didn't say who the new candidate is."

Mr. Locke held his secret in with a little smile until the room became absolutely silent and every eye was on him. "The president of the PAT," he said. "Mr. Grimmet."

"Grimmet!" "Grimmet!" "Grimmet!" The word flickered around the room like the chirping of frogs around a pond.

Mr. Locke tapped the board with his chalk. "All right, let's get to work."

"This is really bad," Jane said as she stood up. The children were moving into their groups, chattering. Everyone was interested in the election again.

Only Bonnie sat alone, slightly stunned. There would be many more grown-ups, now, she was thinking, many more people whose votes she must try to win.

From the back of the room, she could hear Gail analyzing and organizing, still not quite admitting to the class that Bonnie's candidacy was real. "Lucy Ann's committee work with Jane's on the Sitting Station. Jerry, you guys spread out after school and find out if any kid would vote for a Grimmet. Emergency meeting of the Steering Committee at three thirty. In the meantime, don't give up!"

As the class moved off, eager to work, Gail came

over to Bonnie. "Remember your mom said a good campaign can take advantage of anything that happens? 'Be ready,' something like that?"

" 'Readiness is all,' " Bonnie quoted, smiling. "She said."

"Yes. Now we're going to find out how good a campaign we've got. Let me see your speech."

Bonnie shook her head. "Gail, I don't know what to say."

"You don't have it? You've wasted all this time? *Everything* is important now! Your speech could make the whole difference!" Gail was furious. "Work on it, *right now*. Work on it till the Steering Committee meeting, and I'll help you right after. Put in something for the grown-ups, something for the fifth. Remember to end strong."

Bonnie felt entirely confused and helpless—so confused she didn't notice Gail's rudeness, so helpless that even if she had, she wouldn't have taken Gail on now. She needed all the help from Gail that she could get.

"We'll work on it tomorrow and the next day and all weekend if we have to," Gail was saying. "But start!"

With a clean piece of paper in front of her, Bonnie tried to think of what she could possible say to a room full of grown-ups. "1., 2., 3.," she wrote on the paper, "4., 5., 6." As work on the election project hummed all around her, the candidate sat thinking about what Mr. Lipchik had said. She had begun to feel it was her personal responsibility to keep Mrs. Atkins from becoming the permanent principal of Daniel Webster Elementary School. She felt as lonely as an astronaut on the far side of the moon.

16

The Last Meeting of the Steering Committee

By twenty to four, all the Steering Committee but Gail had gathered by the high rock. The trees were bare above, now, the sunlight that came through was without warmth, and the leaves underfoot had a brittle sound.

"How come Gail's late?" Jerry asked. "How come *she* gets to be late?"

"Gail'll come," Jane said. "Bobby, tell us what you figured out."

The new candidacy raised many questions, Bobby explained: How many more parents would come to the meeting? Would kids who might have voted for Bonnie vote for Mr. Grimmet because he might have a better chance of beating Mrs. Atkins? Would any teachers vote for him? Would parents want to vote for a parent? But who could like a Grimmet?

"They elected him PAT president, remember," Bonnie said.

"There were only a few people at the meeting

where he got elected," Jane said. "My mom told me. Nobody else wanted to do it."

"Still, some people might think he's great for that," Jerry said. "The ones who don't know him."

"But do you know anything for sure, Bobby?" Jane asked.

"Okay," Bobby said. "Depending on how many come, it'll be close. But I think this probably is going to help us because it splits the grown-ups' vote."

"But you really don't know," Lucy Ann said.

"No one knows for sure till you add up the votes!" Bobby sounded near tears. "People can vote any crazy way they want to, for any crazy reason they have."

"So all we can do," Jane said, "is work double hard to do what we were going to do anyway: Get every kid we can to come vote—except the ninny fifth graders." Then her voice grew more hopeful: "Here comes Gail."

No one even thought of laughing as they watched Gail Dewksbury run awkwardly across the playground. The days when Gail was someone to whisper and giggle about were long gone.

"Amazing news!" Panting, she leaned her back against the rock, standing on one leg, the other folded with her foot against the rock and her fat notebook resting on her knee. "The fifth-grade Grimmet says most of fifth grade would vote for Bonnie if we agree to trade: Locke for Mrs. Tilley!

Bonnie just has to promise to switch the fifth- and sixth-grade teachers for the rest of the year."

There was a second of silence, then wild cheers, followed by a lot of confusion.

"Wouldn't she vote for her own father?" Lucy Ann asked.

"He's her father, remember," Jerry said. "Would you want your father at school all the time?"

"Explain it, Gail," said Bonnie. "Exactly."

"The fifth grade doesn't like Mrs. Tilley that much," Gail said, "and they do like Locke. So that's it. And if we get the fifth-grade votes, we have a really good chance!"

"The fifth grade deserves Locke."

"Locke deserves the fifth grade! It's perfect!"

"The best part for you, Bonnie," Jane said, "is you won't have to fire Mr. Locke."

Bonnie nodded.

Bobby spun his notebook high in the air. It landed on an edge and popped open; papers slid down the face of the high rock.

"Spill it all out, Bobby baby!" Jerry yelled. "All Mr. Locke's stupid work!"

"Mr. Locke would still be in school," Bonnie said.

"Yeah, but not in *our* class," Lucy Ann said.

"The fifth grade can have him!"

"Teaching them wrong math and everything," Bonnie said.

"They want him, Bonnie." Gail's intense and

careful tone made the others pay attention to what Bonnie was saying.

"They like him, Bonnie," Jerry said. "Everyone would be happy."

"We didn't say happy," Bonnie said. "We said fair, and interesting, and good teaching. It's not fair to give them Mr. Locke, when we know he doesn't really care about teaching."

Gail pressed on. "Isn't it fair to let them have who they want, if we get who we want?"

"It would be so simple."

"It would be so easy."

"It would be wrong." Bonnie spoke slowly, thinking this through for herself as she went: "It's not like he's just boring or strict or rude or disorganized or something. He's a bad teacher. If he's still in the school, Schaffer's going to have to have him."

"That's a long time from now," Jerry said. "Bon?"

"We have to worry about ourselves," Gail said. "This year. For us."

"He'd be teaching the fifth grade wrong math," Bonnie said, "and not even noticing. It's not like he's Mrs. Atkins, and we don't like her but we know her kids really learn. It's not like the way they don't like Mrs. Tilley. Mr. Locke is a bad teacher. I don't think we should agree to it."

The others were quiet.

"Gail?" Bonnie asked. "That trade was your idea, wasn't it?"

Gail didn't answer.

"You offered that deal to the Grimmet without asking us," Bonnie said. "Gail, it's not your election. It's for all of us to decide. This election is important for every kid at D-W."

Gail was clicking her pen.

After a minute, Bonnie whispered fiercely, "I won't do it."

"Sure it would be better to get Locke out of school completely," Gail burst out angrily, "and stop him torturing innocent children. But the fifth-grade votes are our only chance. Isn't it better to have him gone from us to kids who want him, than to make no change at all? You're giving up!"

The others murmured agreement.

"No," Bonnie said. She was ready to cry, but she didn't cry. The fierce and useful temper she had discovered in herself while talking with Mr. Lipchik was in place, ready. For the first time, Bonnie was entirely sure what she stood for and what she had to do. "I'm the candidate. I have to do what's right to win the election, and what's right for after the election. You're wrong, Gail, and I won't do it!"

"No! I'm the campaign manager of this campaign, and I'm telling you!" Gail was screaming. "You're going to throw away our whole chance! You are not cooperating!"

"Cooperating?" Bonnie screamed back. "No, I'm not cooperating! Cooperating isn't the point. What's right is what's important!"

Jerry, Lucy Ann, Jane, and Bobby, stunned and uneasy, moved away from Gail, away from Bonnie, up the rock.

The two girls were yelling at the same time, now, neither listening to the other.

"If it hadn't been for me! . . . " Gail was shouting. "You couldn't even have got started! You couldn't win without me! . . . You're such a goody-goody and so chicken you probably wouldn't even fire him!"

"That's all you care about: you!" Bonnie shouted. "You're trying to use the whole school to get what you want. We've told the other kids how we'd make D-W better. We promised them. Yes, I'm chicken of firing Mr. Locke. I'm *more* chicken of fighting Mrs. Atkins, but I'm going to fight her. I'm going to fight her in a way that's good for the whole school."

"Bonnie's right," Jane said softly. "My brothers are coming up, too, and they'd have to fight Mr. Locke all over again. This is horrible enough. This isn't fun anymore."

After a minute, Jerry said, "No, Gail's right. This is our only hope." He was standing at the top of the rock. "Let's vote. The Steering Committee should vote!"

"Think about the whole rest of our year with Locke!" Gail said. "We're so close!" She leaped away from the rock and turned to face the others, still yelling. "If you throw away our best chance, I won't work on the campaign anymore! If Bonnie won't run, we can run Bobby. Bobby could do it."

"But Bonnie's right," Lucy Ann said.

Everyone looked at Bobby.

Bobby blinked. "Bonnie's right," he said.

Gail clicked her pen so none of the colored tips showed. "I hope you can do it," she said coldly.

Bonnie felt Gail was looking straight at her.

Gail walked across the playground and up the sidewalk. She walked slowly, without looking back, but the five she left behind watched in silence until she had passed the corner house.

When she was out of sight, Bonnie asked, her voice still tense and trembling, "Jerry? Are you going to work with us?"

"Oh, sure," Jerry said, but he sounded grim. "I guess we should at least try."

On Thursday, on Friday, over the whole long weekend, apart from getting the Sitting Station ready, Bonnie and the others found very little to do. Was it because under Gail's leadership they had prepared so well? Bonnie wondered. Or was it because without Gail the others couldn't do anything at all?

Bonnie asked Jane, Shawna, Nancy, and Gillian to come over Friday after school to help her pick out the dress she would wear election night. Looking in the mirror at herself dressed so importantly, Bonnie saw four pairs of eyes staring back at her and not one mouth smiling.

Bonnie and Jane talked frequently, sharing worries, trading news about the many things that seemed to be going wrong.

Mrs. Atkins and Mr. Grimmet were campaigning hard now, and the fifth-grade Grimmet had begun handing out bandage buttons for her father. "The copycat!" Bonnie said. "The rat."

"She's such a rat," Jane said, "her little brother should put her in a cage and take her to kindergarten."

Lucy Ann had picked up the leaflets from the printer on Friday, but Jerry hadn't given her enough money, so she had paid three dollars of her own. "She says if he doesn't pay her back, she won't bring the leaflets Monday night," Bonnie said.

"Lucy Ann is a ninny like I always thought," Jane said. "She wanted pineapple juice at the Sitting Station! Little kids like apple and lemonade. Luckily I did the shopping. Lucy Ann is going to be a horrible mother."

But the worst thing that went wrong—by far—Bonnie learned about at her own dinner table, Saturday night.

Since her candidate had won five days before, Mrs. Mann had been happy and gay and had gone grocery shopping twice. A change in her mother's voice now caused Bonnie to tune in on her parents' conversation.

". . . even for a few weeks! It would be a disgrace. If Grimmet wins this, he'll probably run for school board next. On the basis of no talent whatsoever! That man's ego! . . . "

"You're right," Mr. Mann said. "But what can you do about it?"

"We have till Monday night. We'll just get out the vote for Mrs. Atkins!"

Bonnie felt stunned, as if she had been hit over the head and everything had gone numb, from her brains to her legs. She tried hard to understand exactly what this would mean, but it was hard to concentrate with a numb brain and with her mother urgently planning a few feet away.

"I've made some calls. Quite a few people think the same way. We're going to start a marathon telephoning tonight."

"Mom?" Bonnie said, and she tried to speak calmly. "Aren't you still tired from the other . . . ?" Before she finished the sentence she realized it was hopeless; she had heard the old fighting energy in her mother's voice. She asked, instead, "I'm finished. May I be excused?"

As she was clearing her place and starting upstairs, she heard Mrs. Mann saying, "I'll use everything I know about politics to stop him! We'll get a huge turnout!"

From the privacy of her father's study, Bonnie phoned Jane. But besides giving sympathy, there was nothing Jane could do. "It was our election. We had it all figured out."

"And we had a really good chance to win, because none of them cared."

"And then Mr. Grimmet comes in."

"And then my mom. She's going to get masses of grown-ups there."

After a pause, Jane said, "Why don't you just tell her? You could tell your own mother."

"I can't. Well, I could tell her, but she's got them all working now for Mrs. Atkins. How could she explain it if she asks them to stop? If they know we're really trying to win, they might work even harder." Would even her own mother keep campaigning against her, because it was too important to stop Mr. Grimmet?

All Sunday, whenever Mrs. Mann wasn't using the phone, Bonnie and Jane talked. They got nowhere.

Just before she went to bed Sunday night, Bonnie called Jane one last time.

"It's horrible. I listen and listen, and she's so good at it, and there's nothing we can do."

"Everything is going wrong," Jane said.

"Well, there's one good thing," Bonnie said. She giggled. "Did you hear about the football game? Dad and I had to go pick up a pizza for dinner, and I met Bobby up on the avenue. He said there's a big football game on Monday night, so most of Jerry's committee didn't want to come to the election at all! So Bobby decided to bring a TV downstairs to the

Sitting Station. I told him that was as good as Gail. Jane, he blushed."

"He blushed?"

"He blushed! He said, 'Anything for the cause.' Jane! *I'm* the cause! Oh, Jane!" Then her voice slipped from happiness to despair. "Oh, Jane, what if I mess up? I keep thinking I'm forgetting something."

"I know!"

"All these stupid things."

"We need Gail," Jane said softly.

"We need Gail. My mom's too good. She's going to get a hundred people there for Mrs. Atkins. I wish I hadn't yelled at Gail."

"Bon, you had to yell at her. You were right!"

"I hope she's not so mad she'll do something to mess up the election," Bonnie said.

"She won't," Jane assured her. "You're her only hope for getting rid of Mr. Locke."

"But the way I yelled at her!"

"Bon, you still don't understand yelling. Lots of people yell and are still friends."

"I wish . . . Oh, Jane!" Bonnie whispered. "I remember what I forgot. Gail was supposed to help me write my speech!"

17

Maybe Maybe Maybe

An hour before the PAT meeting was to start, Mrs. Mann was still on the phone, trying to get just one more parent to come vote for Mrs. Atkins.

Bonnie, looking very nice but very pale, decided to leave early and visit her friends in Bobby Roberts's basement on her way to school.

Lucy Ann, Jerry, Jane, Walter, and Shawna, had already set up the various areas of the Sitting Station: blankets and pillows in a corner, places for circle games and reading aloud. On one table there were slips of paper and pencils and a sample ballot box, on another juice and cookies, on another colored pens and a big supply of Bon-Daids. By the door, Lucy Ann had placed a stack of leaflets with a list of issues and a biography of the candidate.

"The Station looks terrific," Bonnie said, handing Jane one of her barrettes.

"There's only one problem," Jane said, handing Bonnie one of hers. "No kids."

They waited, listening to the Roberts family moving about overhead, for a very long time.

"I haven't seen anyone go in." Shawna stood by the front window facing the school. It was dark outside, and the black basement windows reflected the huge and almost empty room.

"*Some* people will come," Walter said. "Since Mr. Grimmet started hanging around school, shaking hands with every parent he . . ."

"He shook mine, too, the ninny," Jane said. "I couldn't get out of the way."

"It was like a real ad for the election," Walter said.

Jerry came back from the school. "First, they have the so-called entertainment by the orchestra, then some stuff about spring fair, then Mr. Locke is going to explain the project. Then the election. I'll come tell you when it's time to bring them."

"Bring who?" Lucy Ann asked.

As if responding to this cue, three first graders came rushing, shouting, down the steps. "Hey, where's the lemonade?" "Where's the selection?" Happy to be needed at last, the sixth graders went to work. Soon it was as if the 8:45 bell had rung and children were pouring in from the playground.

Shawna stayed by the window awhile longer, watching dark silhouettes approach the lighted doorway of the school. "A lot of grown-ups are going straight in, not bringing kids. Lots."

"Maybe they have older kids," Jane said. "Maybe

their kid's in the orchestra, and they'll go home when the music's over."

"Maybe. Maybe. Maybe!" Lucy Ann said. "I wish I knew!" She was helping children practice voting, writing on a ballot, then folding it to keep the name secret as they put it in the box.

"I'm good at folding," a third grader said.

"Why are you so good at folding?" Lucy Ann asked.

"From passing notes," the third grader said. "We just started this year. We fold them teeny-tiny so Mrs. Atkins can't see."

"Good practice for being a good citizen," Jane said, grinning at Bonnie.

But Bonnie couldn't smile; the scared feeling was coming back. "I'd better go now," she said. Through the window, the school looked far away.

"Did you work on your speech again?" Jane asked softly.

Bonnie nodded.

The night before, she and Jane had quickly put together a list of every point she must mention. Bonnie had worked on it now and then all day, but every time she wrote a sentence, then read it aloud, it sounded so stupid she had crossed it out. Just before supper, she had gone to her father's study and typed a careful outline of what she wanted to say. She would speak from that. Either it would work or it wouldn't, she told Jane. "But I just couldn't write it."

"That's fine," Jane said calmly. "Remember, you don't have to get every word right, you just have to say what you mean."

Bonnie shrugged. She still couldn't believe that in less than an hour she would be making a speech to more than a hundred people.

"And remember it doesn't have to be long." Jane turned and handed a piece of Bonnie literature to a second-grade parent who was just leaving. "I hope you'll vote for Bonnie Mann," Jane said. "The sixth grade thinks she would do a great job."

"Thanks," the mother said. "I might just do that."

Blushing, Bonnie raced up the basement stairs.

She found the second-floor hall noisy and full; the drawings and stories along the walls were mostly hidden by parents and teachers standing and talking. Mr. Lipchik was still bringing extra chairs from the classrooms. Behind the little row of chairs at the front hung the PAT banner: "Your PAT Standing Together for Excellence in Education." Mrs. Atkins, a flower pinned to her dress, greeted parents at the door. Mr. Grimmet, wearing a bright bow tie, walked about introducing himself to people he didn't know.

A small group of sixth graders huddled together. They looked, Bonnie thought, as shy and uncomfortable as she and Schaffer when they were allowed to stay up late for a very grown-up party. She went to stand safely among them, tying and untying the three velvet bows on the front of her dress.

"I didn't expect so many . . ." said Nancy, looking around.

"It's weird they're all here, in our hall and with our rooms all dark . . . and our election."

"It's their election, too," Walter said. "That's the trouble."

"Bonnie, you're so nervous, you're going to faint," said Jerry. "Let's walk around." They went over to where Miss Boyard was fussing with the piles of ballots and the ballot boxes.

"Hi!" Jerry said. "Why are you here?"

"I'm part of the D-W community, aren't I? Besides, the rest of you may be voting for your principal; I'm voting for my boss!" Before she moved away, she gave Bonnie a wink so slight it seemed her eyelid merely twitched.

"Did . . . ?" Bonnie whispered to Jerry, and Jerry whispered back, "Yeah!"

Gillian and Nancy came running up, their faces anxious: "It's ten minutes late, and they're still coming in!"

My mom sure did a great job, Bonnie thought.

There were not many children in the hall. Most of the sixth graders and the young children were over at the Sitting Station. There were a few third graders and quite a few fifth graders here and there.

"Where are the fourth graders?" Gillian asked.

"I see a few," Bonnie said. "But they're all for us! Are they at the Sitting Station?"

"A couple are helping," Jerry said. "We should have paid more attention to the fourth, to be sure they all came."

"There's nothing we can do about it now," Nancy said, grimly.

Would Gail have made sure the fourth came out to vote, Bonnie wondered, if she had been working the last few days? As the others talked, Bonnie forced herself to get the situation straight, as Gail would have. Most of the fourth hadn't come, most of the fifth probably wouldn't vote for her, which made the third-grade votes very important. But the third graders were afraid Mrs. Atkins would know if they didn't vote for her. The kids' vote situation did not look good.

"Is Gail here?" Jerry asked.

"I don't know if she's even coming."

"Tough on her!" Gillian suddenly spun around. "Oh, Bonnie! I can't wait to hear your speech! Is it all ready?"

"You've asked me three times, Gilly!" Bonnie snapped. "I'm going to see my parents." She headed toward the back, where Mr. and Mrs. Mann were enjoying the rare chance to talk quietly together.

"You look terrific, dear," Bonnie's mother said and gave her a hug.

"This is your big moment, Bon," Mr. Mann said, and winked.

Bonnie nodded without pleasure. "Did you bring Schaffer?"

"He's over with Jane."

Her father moved to the next chair and patted the seat he had left empty. Bonnie sat. More than anything in the world, she wished she could stay between her mother and father, daydreaming to the safe, comfortable sound of their conversation. But when she actually listened, what they were talking about was far from comforting.

Her mother was pleased with how many people had come and was confident that Mrs. Atkins would win easily. She was quite distressed, however, about her previous candidate; the new city council member was not selecting his staff or setting up his office or preparing his program, as Mrs. Mann had wished.

Trying not to hear any of this, Bonnie looked around the hall. She wondered if all the adults had already made up their minds. She smiled to Jane's parents.

. "Things are different, after you're in," her father said to her mother. "You just can't expect to do everything you'd hoped to."

Bonnie looked down at the marked-up page·of her speech notes. There were not more than forty words. "Mom? Am I making too many promises? Things I wouldn't be able to do?"

"Bonnie, my heart, my favorite candidate of all! Promise! Dream! People want to know what you care about. If you were elected," she said with a smile that was slightly sad, "you'd do your best."

Gail came into the hall, then, and Bonnie watched her so intently, she barely heard her mother's words.

"The most important thing, Bonnie," Mrs. Mann said, "is that good people will take on the work of government, that good people are willing to run for public office."

Gail stood in the doorway, looking carefully around. Her glance touched everything and settled on nothing. After a moment, she sat in the back row and began to read. She turned her pages slowly, as if she had no interest in her surroundings, as if this was simply a pleasant place to read a very gripping story.

Behind Gail, Bonnie saw more grown-ups streaming into the hall. Mom did a great job, she thought. If only she had been working for me.

18

A Great Little School

Bonnie heard Mr. Grimmet introduce himself to the parents with whom Mrs. Atkins was talking. "If you're ready, Mrs. Atkins," he said, "we might begin. We have a lot of young people here tonight, and we have to think of getting them home."

"Whenever you're ready, Mr. Grimmet," Mrs. Atkins replied. "We're all here for the good of the children. I don't think this need take long." The rivals walked to the front of the room together, smiling, turning to the parents on either side, nodding, smiling again.

"They're going up," Mr. Mann said gently. "Good luck, Bon."

"Good luck with your speech!" Mrs. Mann said. "Win or lose, Hon, I'm proud of you."

Bonnie nodded and tried to smile. At the front, she sat at one end of the row of chairs facing the audience and was grateful to Walter, Jerry, Nancy, and Gillian for sitting in the front row, opposite her. But though they were just a few feet away, she felt a vast distance between them. No comforting whisper, no folded note, could reach her where she sat on display. Before I'm back with my friends, she thought, we'll know who won.

Mr. Grimmet waited until Mrs. Atkins was seated, then turned to the audience and rapped his gavel lightly to call the meeting to order. "Good evening. It's good to see so many of you here tonight. One reason Daniel Webster is a special school is that this community truly cares about its children.

"Since it would not be proper for me to have a double role this evening, I will soon turn the gavel over to the vice-president of the PAT. But because our music program is very dear to me, I'm going to indulge myself first in the privilege of introducing our wonderful orchestra."

He went on for a while, and then the orchestra went on for a while, and then the vice-president of the PAT asked Mrs. Atkins to make a few remarks about the late Miss Cherry.

"Hey . . . no fair!" Jerry spoke so loudly, Bonnie made a *shhh!* sign with her mouth. He didn't notice. "They both get to talk twice."

"There's nothing we can do about it now." Nancy's voice was even louder.

Mrs. Atkins's slow, firm, careful voice added to Bonnie's growing anxiety. She sat fuming about Mrs. Atkins's great power over her class. If only there was a way to convince the third graders that they could safely vote however they wanted.

Bonnie sat upright so fast her chair thumped.

Mrs. Atkins paused in midsentence, turned, and gave Bonnie a lengthy, corrective frown.

Bonnie sat still for just a moment, but she knew that no matter what Mrs. Atkins did about it, she had to get over to the Sitting Center. She stood.

Mrs. Atkins turned again, wearing an expression of exaggerated surprise.

"I'll be right back," Bonnie mumbled. "Excuse me, please."

Mrs. Atkins pressed her lips together, and Nancy, Gillian, Walter, and Jerry watched anxiously as their candidate turned and went out through the doors just behind her seat.

Bonnie raced down the stairs, enjoying her sudden freedom and eager to put her idea to work. Leaning on the banister, she skipped every other stair, until she met three mothers walking up. She quickly smiled and slowed to a ladylike walk. Stupid! she told herself. They're not going to vote for me because of the way I walk. They're going to vote for him or her, anyway. That's why they're here. She broke into a run.

The Robertses' basement was now an orderly bedlam. Small children were dancing in a circle, sitting and clapping to a song, playing Simon Says. Small children were marking practice ballots, listening to Mrs. Roberts read a story, giggling under a table. Children were in line at the Bon-Daid table, in line for lemonade. Some older kids were cheering on their football team, and a very few, very young ones were curled up in blankets, not so much asleep as dazed.

Bonnie found Jane by the door. "I need Schaffer. Where's Schaffer?"

Jane pointed. "I think something's going on. He's acting funny."

Bonnie went to where her brother was whispering in a corner with the third-grade Grimmet. "Schaffer?"

He looked at her suspiciously.

"Could I talk to you for a minute?"

The Grimmet frowned at her and left.

"What's going on?"

Schaffer said nothing.

"I mean it. *What's* going on?"

Slowly, Schaffer turned sideways and pulled open his pants pocket so Bonnie could see inside. She saw what looked like a very fat roll of dollar bills.

"What's that for?"

Schaffer coughed an important cough. "If you don't know it," he said, "this election is very important. We could get a soccer coach."

He tells *me* it's important! Bonnie thought. "What's it *for*?"

"I'm going to get you some votes," he said. "I'm going to give it—a one, a five, a ten, a twenty, a fifty, a hundred, a five hundred, brand-new Monopoly money—to certain kids I know."

"No!" Bonnie said. "Listen! A lot of grown-ups won't like it if I win. If they find out even one vote was bought, they would cancel the results. Besides, Schafe, if you care, it's wrong."

"It's just a prize," he said. "I'm just giving it."

Bonnie thought very carefully about what she would say next. "Schaffer Mann, if you give out any money at all, even one bill, then I promise you— and this is a campaign promise, and I will keep it— I promise you that if I'm elected, I will *not* get a soccer coach and you will be doing jumping jacks from now to junior high!"

Schaffer looked at the ground. "Okay."

"And that goes for the Grimmet, too. Tell him."

"Okay!" he said. "Don't yell."

"And Schaffer? If you really want me to win, if you really want to help, find every third grader here and tell them the ballots really *are* secret. Tell them Mrs. Atkins can't see in their heads, and she can't see in their ballots. She will never know how they voted. It's their secret. Maybe if *you* tell them, they'll believe it."

"Okay!" He walked slowly away, but in a moment he was back to ask, "How'd you know I was going to give the money?"

"I'm practicing to be the principal," Bonnie said, and headed for the door, her errand done.

Feeling a hundred percent better, she entered the school and started back upstairs.

Mr. Locke came running down. "See you tomorrow, Bon," he said, going right on by her.

Bonnie stared. "Aren't you staying?"

He stopped. "Oh, I've done my part. I've just explained the Experience in Democracy. The parents were very impressed."

"Aren't you going to be here for . . . ?"

"Oh. I'm sorry I can't stay to hear you, but I have to . . ." His voice faded.

"For the vote, I mean," Bonnie said. "Don't you want to vote?"

"I'm sure Mrs. Atkins will do fine without my vote."

"I mean—don't you even want to see . . . ?"

But even with the election project, Mr. Locke didn't really care. "I do have to go," he said, looking at his watch. "So long." He waved to her, without looking, and continued down.

A feeling of disgust came over Bonnie. "Mr. Locke!" she called.

He stopped running and looked up at her through the railings.

"Do you understand?" she asked.

Mr. Locke looked puzzled and put his hand to his ear.

"Do you really understand?"

Frowning, he shook his head, and put his hand to his ear again, and shrugged, and ran on.

"Good-bye," Bonnie said, "Mr. Locke."

She got back to her seat just in time to hear Walter

speak her name. She was glad she had been nominated last, and so would be the last to speak.

The vice-president introduced the first candidate.

"Good evening. I want especially to welcome the young people here tonight," Mrs. Atkins said. "The excellent and imaginative Exercise in Democracy is an example of what a fine teacher, a creative and innovative teacher like Mr. Locke, can do in a stable and confident environment."

Mrs. Atkins stood with her elbows at her side and her hands clasped over her belt. "We teach our children to be good citizens, and I know they will make their ballots count for the very best for Daniel Webster.

"About tonight's election, my remarks will be brief. Daniel Webster has always stood for the very best in American education. I'm proud to report to you that your school is in excellent shape."

Here she was interrupted by enthusiastic applause, and she smiled graciously before going on.

"For the sake of the children, during this interim period we need as principal someone who knows the school well, who knows every child and every program, who will be here every day.

"Our children deserve to learn and develop in a stable and confident environment. That has been my goal, and that, I hope, has been my achievement. How many times have you heard me say it? Our Children Are Our Future."

Bonnie felt a guilty shiver as Mrs. Atkins correctly and distinctly enunciated "Our" and "Are."

"I ask for your vote tonight, to permit me to keep doing the work I know and love best, teaching and serving the parents and children of Daniel Webster Elementary School. Thank you."

There was a good deal of clapping as Mrs. Atkins sat down. Mr. Grimmet quickly stood and waved into the dying applause.

"I believe in management!" he began. "That is the reason, and the only reason, I would even consider running against our beloved friend." He smiled at Mrs. Atkins, and Mrs. Atkins smiled back. "The management expertise I can offer is why I am a candidate tonight.

"You know me as president of your PAT, but I'm also vice-president at Triple Smith. I know management. I know budget. I can make the tough decisions. Over seventy people work for me, and I . . ."

Bonnie's mind, and her eyes, were soon wandering. She saw a father still in his office clothes rush in and find a seat. She quickly looked down at her speech paper. She studied it for a moment, then unfolded it and looked inside. There were still no more than forty words. She was going to have to make up all the rest. She tried to prepare her first sentence, but her mind went blank.

Her mind simply stayed blank, paying no atten-

tion to her speech or Mr. Grimmet's, not tuning in
again until he was finishing.

"We have the opportunity tonight, ladies and
gentlemen," he was saying, "and you young people
here, the wonderful Expedition into Democracy, the
opportunity, in all modesty, to elect, on a short-
term basis, a long-range planner. Planning saves
money—perhaps enough to give our children the
special courses they deserve. Let's get these kids a
soccer coach!"

There were loud cheers. Walter and Gillian and
Jerry murmured furiously: ". . . our issue!"

"There's nothing we can do about it now," Nancy
said.

"We're already giving our kids a great education.
We all know that. I ask your vote to improve the
only part of Webster that needs improvement: management. Thank you."

The applause for Mr. Grimmet's speech soon
faded into an awkward silence.

Bonnie stood, still and silent, hidden by the podium until Mr. Lipchik brought over a plastic milk
crate. "Tonight," he said, "you'd better let everyone
take a good look at you."

"Thank you," she whispered, then stepped up to
face the crowd. She looked around, aware especially
of the fifth graders watching her, fifth graders whose
vote she had one last chance to win.

"Good evening," she thought. I should start with

"Good evening." I've never said "Good evening" in my whole life!

Her nervous throat swallowed the "Good," so her speech began simply, "Evening." Oh, well, she thought, that's the way Mr. Lipchik says it. She saw him smile to her from where he leaned against the fourth-grade door, and she was able to go on a little more bravely.

"The sixth grade's election project is a real project. We have some good ideas for Daniel Webster." She said softly, but clearly, *"So we really are asking you to vote for me."*

There were a few mutters of surprise, but only a few adults understood immediately that the real drama of the evening was not the contest between Mrs. Atkins and Mr. Grimmet, but the challenge of the determined candidate from sixth grade.

"We know it's not usual to have a kid be principal. But it is legal, and you can check your bylaws on that. If you think it's weird, well, it *is* weird, but you'll probably get used to the idea, like I did. Remember it's only a few weeks until the new year, and a lot of that time is vacation. So you don't need to worry."

"Now, wait a minute!" A father rose slowly to his feet, interrupting her. "You mean you *really* expect us to vote for a sixth grader as principal?"

"Yes," Bonnie said, in a rather small voice.

"So the kids can play all day? That's like putting

the fox to guard the chickens!" The father laughed, as did quite a few others.

"No!" Bonnie said. "No. We wouldn't just play. We know we have to work. But we would change some things. We want our school to be interesting, and also fair, and also to have good teaching." Bonnie checked some faces, fifth graders' faces, parents' faces; she couldn't tell if she was having any effect. "Mrs. Atkins and Mr. Grimmet say D-W is so good, but the sixth grade thinks some things here are wrong, and we think a lot of things should be better."

The father was still standing. "You say you're so interested in education, but may I ask, young lady"—and here he paused and looked around, smiling—"how you, yourself, would get an education if you're spending your time in the principal's office? Isn't your first responsibility to your own work?"

Several parents clapped loud and long.

"Sir," Bonnie said, "we have thought about that a lot, and we have figured out some ways. I can skip recess, and anyway, Mrs. Atkins teaches her class and is principal at the same time. But the main reason I don't worry that I might not get educated while I'm principal is, well, I'm not getting such a great education now. So what's the difference?"

There were loud murmurs then, and the father started to respond, but Bonnie leaned forward. "Maybe you could please wait until I tell you our ideas; then if you think our ideas would make D-W better, you can vote for me."

"Let her talk!" someone yelled.

With a flood of relief, with a spurt of joy, Bonnie recognized her mother's voice.

Other parents also let the father know they wanted to hear Bonnie. He shrugged and sat down.

Bonnie glanced at her paper.

"One, we want the lunchroom to be decent."

The sixth graders in the front row groaned with embarrassment, and Bonnie could sense Mrs. Atkins's eyebrows rising. She went on.

"The lunchroom has been bad since I was in first grade. Everybody hates it, fifth and sixth and everybody. We need to fix it.

"Two, we need good teaching—teachers who explain and don't make fun of kids who don't understand. We need good math in the sixth grade. That's important, and we don't have it now. Kids who want to be astronauts or politicians or veterinarians"— Bonnie sighed—"or practically anything have to know math."

There was loud applause from the back of the room. Bonnie was sure *that* was her father, but quite a few others joined him.

"And the second graders need to learn to write," she went on. "They shouldn't have to wait for next year with Mrs. Atkins to learn. Some sixth graders have been tutoring them, and we know they can do it.

"Three, we want a soccer coach, like Mr. Grimmet said. A lot of our P.E. is really stupid. We want hard games with good equipment and real rules and a chance to get better.

"Four, we need things to be fixed and safe to use around here, so we know the teachers and the parents care about us. Mr. Lipchik keeps the school going, but they keep telling him reasons why he has to wait to do things. You might not have noticed but those two swings still aren't fixed—from last spring! The kids know it.

"Five, we want to make school more interesting. We want . . ."

The father was up again, holding up his hand like a policeman to stop her. "Now, please," he said. "Please! What does that mean—make school more ineresting?" He shook his head and sat back down.

"Well, it's hard to explain, exactly, but . . . You all tell us education is so important, and school is so good, but then when we come here every day, a lot of what we do is so dumb. We know we have to memorize the times tables and spelling, but also we would like to find out more about real things, like at the astronaut assembly. We want to *do* more real things. The teachers always saw we have to get ready: ready for fifth grade, ready for sixth, ready for junior high. 'Readiness is all,' they say; they say it all the time. But when are we ever going to *be* there and start doing something real?

"The best thing we did this year was the election

project: We worked hard, and we learned a lot. We don't know what's going to happen, but whatever happens, it will be real.

"Six, we want fair rules, fair for everybody, so we won't feel so insulted all the time. Teachers and children are different, but most rules should be the same for both, like nobody being rude to anybody, and no drinking coffee or eating in class."

There was some applause at this, and Bonnie decided to end her list there. She knew she already had the votes of anyone who cared about small children having plenty of small mammals. "So those are our ideas. And if you . . ."

A mother was standing, already talking. "Well, you certainly have made some useful points, Bonnie. But what makes you think a child could do a better job on all this than a trained and experienced professional educator?"

"Well, see, that's the thing. *No* one *is* doing anything about any of this stuff. We've complained about sixth-grade math, and lots of kids have asked for better P.E., and everyone knows about the lunchroom and the swings. But nothing gets better. Sometimes they say they're working on it, and we should be good citizens and be polite and wait. But . . ."

Bonnie was having a hard time, herself, worrying about being polite. She took a deep breath.

"I'm not sure being a good citizen *is* being polite

every time, I'm not sure it *means* always being co-operative and doing everything you're told. If teachers boss kids around and are rude to us and don't listen to what *we* say, and then they tell us we have to sit quietly and do whatever *they* say, and we shouldn't even ask why . . . that's like what King George told the American colonists, Mrs. Atkins. Just like King George!"

Bonnie grinned, the other sixth graders laughed, and Mrs. Atkins looked slightly puzzled.

"Also, I don't think *you're* being a good citizen to keep telling us you're working on it, and then nothing happens. All that just keeps things the way they are, and we need some things to change."

From the deep, almost breathless, silence in the long hall, Bonnie could tell that right now she was doing the worst thing she had ever done. Writing with tomato soup on the lunch table was nothing to this. Facing up to Mrs. Atkins in front of everyone was the worst thing, and the most right, and the best thing, she had ever done in her whole life.

She dared herself to look at Mrs. Atkins, then, and she did look, and Mrs. Atkins did not seem pleased.

"In fact, Mr. Locke is *not* a fine teacher, and in fact, Mrs. Atkins knows it because she is tutoring him in math. And in fact, Mr. Locke *didn't* think up the election project, a kid did, a smart kid in our class, Gail Dewksbury. And in fact, the sixth grade doesn't want Mr. Locke to be our teacher anymore."

Bonnie glanced at Mr. Lipchik and thought, There! Now you see how bad I can be.

"Please think about these ideas before you vote. Our ideas could stop a big waste of your money. A great student of history once said"—and here Bonnie grinned to Mr. Lipchik—"Any teacher who takes your tax money for teaching math—and doesn't teach it—is a scalawag!"

The tension broke, then, with gasps of surprise and laughter.

"Well, do you want to keep spending your taxes on a scalawag teacher who doesn't teach?" Bonnie shouted.

"No!" "No!" came from many places, and the "no"s quickly blended into a mean and happy roar.

Not everyone was laughing, of course. Bonnie could see many parents talking seriously, indignantly, furiously.

But she was overjoyed to see Mr. Lipchik stomping one foot and nodding, his nose wrinkled up in a kind of silent laughter. She was thrilled to see Gail standing at the back of the crowd, her face grim but her hands high over her head clapping in a slow, firm rhythm.

Suddenly, Bonnie felt wonderful. She was saying just what she wanted to say, she was right, the speech was good, many people were applauding, and Gail was with them, after all.

When the audience was quiet again, she finished:

"Every kid here knows some way D-W should be better. Probably every parent and every teacher knows some way, too, if you would just think about it instead of always saying it's a good little school.

"We hope you will give us the chance to start making Daniel Webster into a *great* little school! Thank you."

Bonnie's friends jumped up, clapping and cheering, and Jerry raced for the exit. Applause began to sound all over the hall.

On her way back to her seat, Bonnie looked straight at Mrs. Atkins, locking onto her gaze like radar that has found the enemy. Mrs. Atkins, just as firmly, stared back.

19

"Vote for the Kid"

As the applause went on, Bonnie shrank back into her chair. She flashed a quick grin to her friends, then stepped over to the front row for just a moment, to jump up and down with Gilly.

Mr. Grimmet and Mrs. Atkins, who had at first clapped politely, now moved restlessly in their seats. In another moment, Mrs. Atkins stood up decisively and walked back to the podium, where she nudged the milk carton out of the way with her toe and held up her hands for quiet.

"Bonnie is apparently unaware that both Miss Cherry and I have worked diligently to obtain the parts for the broken swings," she said. "There are budgetary considerations and procedural obstacles in the central administration. Her lack of understanding simply demonstrates how inappropriate it would be to put an inexperienced person in the demanding job of principal.

"I also want to inform the parents whose children

don't eat at school that we have recently had a few problems with the lunchroom. We have been working on this, and the situation is already much improved."

She finished with a confident smile, but her confidence was ill-founded. The attention of the audience, once the applause stopped, had not been on her words.

Another sound was growing louder by the moment, a rhythmic sound, ominous and powerful as the crash of distant ocean waves: the sound of many voices chanting, of many, many feet marching in unison. What the voices were chanting, it soon became clear, was:

> Vote for the Kid!
> Vote for the Kid!
> Bonnie for Principal!
> Vote for the Kid!

Wow! Bonnie thought, they got the slogan! Just in time! She could see parents, probably those who had left their sons and daughter at the Sitting Station, murmuring anxiously.

The chant grew louder, and the tread of feet took on extra force from stomping up the stairs.

Mrs. Atkins nodded to the vice-president and sat down. The vice-president rapped her gavel and said something no one heard.

Then, as the roar reached the door to the upstairs hall, there was sudden and complete silence. Parents and teachers turned in their seats.

Jerry and Bobby opened the double doors and held them wide. In walked Jane, and behind her fifty, perhaps sixty, children, small and large. They moved quickly to the front and sat on the floor.

"I have never seen that child sit so still before," remarked four mothers and three fathers about seven different children.

Bonnie was thrilled to see that every child had— on the back of a hand, on a cheek, smack in the center of a forehead—a bandage bearing some form of the letter "B."

"Are they hurt?" she heard someone ask somebody.

"Couldn't be. Not every single one of them."

"B for Band-Aid?" somebody asked someone.

"B for Bonnie, I believe."

The long hall now held over two hundred people. Mr. Grimmet moved closer to Mrs. Atkins, whispering earnestly.

The vice-president of the PAT now explained the voting procedures: After the ballots were passed out, each voter would write the name of one candidate on the ballot, fold it, and place it in the ballot boxes.

The vice-president, consulting her copy of the bylaws, was particularly careful to mention that "Every member of the school community may participate in such a special election."

Hearing those words again, realizing now how very dangerous they were, Mrs. Atkins and Mr. Grimmet looked at each other.

"There's nothing they can do about it now," said Nancy loudly, and hearing her, Bonnie's heart surged with hope.

Then she noticed Bobby Roberts standing by the side wall paying no attention to the proceedings, but counting, just counting and counting and writing his numbers down. He was counting, she was sure, the number of adults and the number of children, and he looked worried.

The vice-president went on to explain how the votes would be counted. "The ballot boxes will be taken to the reading lab. The PAT treasurer, secretary, and I will do the counting. The PAT president and the acting principal won't take their usual part, since they are candidates, but they will be present as observers. Are there any questions?"

Bonnie was a little uneasy when Gail Dewksbury stood. "Shouldn't the third candidate and a representative of the sixth-grade election project be at the counting?" she asked.

"I believe you misunderstand," the vice-president said. "Mrs. Atkins and Mr. Grimmet will not be there as candidates, but because of their official positions."

"But they *are* candidates. It's not fair that the third candidate isn't there, too, if the other two are," Gail said. "Also, the election project has an official part in this election."

"Not fair!" called a voice from the back. "Not fair!" "Not fair!" Twenty, thirty voices echoed the words.

The vice-president looked for guidance to Mr. Grimmet. Mr. Grimmet looked to Mrs. Atkins. Mrs. Atkins strode to the podium once again. On her face was an expression Bonnie recognized, an expression Mrs. Atkins used frequently in the first weeks of school as she made clear to her class the boundaries of appropriate behavior.

Her voice matched her face. "May I ask what purpose would be served by having a sixth grader present? The outcome of this election will be a matter of simple fact. Five responsible citizens surely are capable of counting a few hundred ballots accurately."

"Having a sixth grader there," Gail said, "might make sure the counting is accurate."

There were gasps here and there around the room.

"Gail? May I ask what you are suggesting?"

"Our calculations," Gail said, "show that this vote is going to be very close. We want to be sure every ballot is counted, even the ones where the handwriting is messy or the name isn't spelled right."

Once more, Gail had brought up something no one else had even imagined, and Bonnie was grateful.

A father stood up: "One of the complaints the

students apparently have is that some children haven't been taught to write well. That's no secret to second-grade parents, though I guess till now most of us thought it was only our own child who was having trouble at D-W. It would be unjust if those kids couldn't make things better for themselves because of that very problem. Let's be fair about this."

Quite a few parents clapped loudly. The second graders themselves cheered, perhaps because of their passion to write, perhaps because they liked to hear themselves discussed at this important meeting.

"I should have explained to the sixth graders," Mrs. Atkins said, "that we would welcome their representative at the counting as a logical conclusion of their classroom exercise, but the reading lab is, unfortunately, very small."

"Mrs. Atkins!" Mrs. Tilley jumped to her feet, jingling her keys. "I'd be happy to unlock the fifth-grade room, right across the hall."

"Thank you, Mrs. Tilley," Bonnie said.

"Thank you," Mrs. Atkins said, "Mrs. Tilley."

"Yeah, Mrs. Tilley!" yelled one small child. "Vote for the Kid!"

"Shhhh!" said several others.

Mrs. Atkins was again seated. The vice-president, with only shouts of "Fair!" to guide her, announced that Bonnie Mann could be present at the vote counting and could appoint an observer from the election project.

Immediately, Bonnie stood. "I appoint the sixth-grade class president, Bobby Roberts."

The vice-president ordered the ballots passed out and the voting to begin. The hall was filled with chatter and shouts.

Two fourth graders came running up to Bonnie. "That was good!" said one.

"That was a good speech," said the other.

"Thank you," Bonnie said.

"Mrs. Atkins will have to get us a soccer coach now!" They ran off, and Bonnie stared after them, flabbergasted. She wondered if they would even vote for her.

Was there really no hope that she could win? At the last minute, would voting for a child for principal seem so weird, so bold, that not one kid, even her friends, would dare to write her name on the ballots? She remembered a horrible fantasy she had had in which the final count was 167 votes for Mrs. Atkins and just one vote for her, so everyone knew that the one vote was Bonnie's own.

She looked at the ballot in her hand, her confidence suddenly gone. Hoping for a sign, she searched the noisy crowd.

Many adults stood quietly holding their blank ballots, looking toward the candidates at the front of the room. The kindergarteners and first and second graders, ballots on the floor, bottoms in the air, labored to fit their printing onto the small pieces of paper. The third graders compared folding methods.

The older children were already fooling around in line as they waited to put their ballots in the box.

She saw Mr. Lipchik watching her from where he stood near the ballot box. She looked down at her ballot. It had been folded and refolded and folded again, although she had not yet written her choice.

Mr. Lipchik came over. "Did you like what you said?"

Bonnie nodded.

"Would you vote for you if it weren't yourself?"

Bonnie nodded, and Mr. Lipchik walked away.

After she had put her ballot in the box, Bonnie found Bobby. "I saw you counting," she said. "How many?"

"About eighty kids, about a hundred thirty grown-ups."

"What does that mean?"

"If all the kids vote for you, which they won't, and if the grown-ups split between Mrs. Atkins and Mr. Grimmet, which they won't, then you would win. Okay, but they won't." Bobby said this kindly, and Bonnie nodded.

"If most of the grown-ups vote for him or for her," Lucy Ann said, "they've got it."

"It'll be her," Walter said. "Hardly anybody clapped for him."

"The ninny," Nancy said. "He made the parents notice the election, so a lot more came, then he gave such a nerdy speech, they'll all vote for Mrs. Atkins."

"So if we lose, it's because of the Grimmet," Jane said. Bonnie was grateful that Jane didn't say, And also because of Mrs. Mann.

"I bet some grown-ups vote for Bonnie," Gillian said. "Lots of them clapped for her."

"That doesn't mean anything," Walter said. "It's like when they cheer for the hero in a movie. It doesn't mean they'd do something brave themselves, like vote for the kid."

Bonnie's parents came pushing through the little crowd around their daughter, and both hugged her at once.

"Bonnie! Love! I'm so sorry," Mrs. Mann said.

"That's okay, Mom. You didn't know."

"I didn't know. We've been talking to everyone now, everyone we could, trying to catch them before they voted. . . ."

"Come on, Bonnie," Bobby said. "They're going in for the count."

20
It

The first time, Bonnie didn't believe it, and no one looked at her.

The second time, she and Bobby glanced at each other, and quickly looked away. None of the adults looked up from the piles of little papers, and they immediately began counting again. Bobby stepped right up to the table, bumping it slightly. Mrs. Atkins frowned, but neither Mrs. Atkins nor Bobby took their eyes off the hands that were counting the votes.

But when, for the third time, the totals were thirty-one for Mr. Grimmet, ninety for Mrs. Atkins, and ninety-one for Bonnie, Bonnie's head began to nod, her jaw slowly dropped into a wide, open-mouthed grin, and some rather strange gurgly noises came from deep in her throat.

The PAT secretary repeated the numbers.

There was a pause.

"Well," Mrs. Atkins said. She coughed. She stood. She took her right hand from her belt and held it out. "Congratulations." She shook Bonnie's hand.

"Thank you." Bonnie looked Mrs. Atkins in the eye, really looked her in the eye, for the second time in her life. Her smile was still growing, but by now Mrs. Atkins had started for the door. The other adults quickly hurried after her.

"Hey!" Bobby was hardly able to speak through his own huge grin. "We'd better look serious."

Bonnie hid her foolish face by staying directly behind Bobby as the counting committee walked from Mrs. Tilley's classrooom back into the hall. The sound of that hallful of people growing quiet as suddenly as if a gong had been struck helped Bonnie get her expression under control. She managed to stay inconspicuous until the vice-president read out the totals.

But when a shriek went up from the children, a shriek made the more vivid by the shocked silence of the adults, her grin burst out again. Bonnie felt as if her head were a balloon with a happy face painted on it, floating light and giddy above a body that was itself none too firmly connected to the ground.

The applause grew. No one heard the vice-president tap her gavel to end the meeting. Sixth graders raced up to hug Bonnie and each other in one huge, jumping mass. Soon all the children were racing around, hugging, shouting, asking Bonnie to autograph their sneakers, their Bon-Daids, their campaign leaflets.

The adults began to move slowly from group to group, inventing and repeating words, phrases, and sentences, trying to explain to themselves what had happened. Most were talking, and very few listened. Bonnie saw Mrs. Atkins standing with three third-grade parents who were murmuring angrily, her own lips clamped shut.

"Mrs. Atkins is trying her mature best to act appropriately," Mr. Lipchik said, as he picked up some chairs near Bonnie. "The truth is the lady's mad, which, come to think of it, *is* appropriate. It might be tactful to leave the adults alone. Give them time to adjust."

Bonnie nodded. With the help of the Steering Committee, she rounded up the boisterous children and herded them toward the door.

Before she could go outside herself, however, Mrs. Tilley came up to her. "Congratulations, Bonnie! We've needed to change some of these things for years, but . . . Well, it was hard to get anything going. I want to help. Just call on me. Please."

Right behind Mrs. Tilley was the second-grade father who had spoken up. "Lots of parents would like to help, too, Bonnie. Would you like us to form a new parents' council to help you get these changes under way?" He nodded to Mrs. Tilley. "With the teachers, of course."

"To work with my Steering Committee," Bonnie said. "Yes, that would be good." She took down his name and phone number. "Thanks," she said. "Thanks, Mrs. Tilley."

Then Mr. Grimmet came blustering up to Bonnie, shaking and shaking her hand while he smiled at everyone else. Bonnie found it hard to believe this ninny of a man was vice-president of an important company. "As president of the PAT, I want to congratulate you on this extraordinary victory. If there's anything . . ."

"Mr. Grimmet!" Bonnie said. "May I ask you a question?" She led him into a corner where they talked privately for a few minutes, then Bonnie started for the door again, even happier than before.

But now Gail was waiting. A little uncomfortably, they congratulated each other, then Gail got right to the point: "You're going to have to fire Locke right away, before they . . ."

"I already took care of Mr. Locke," Bonnie said quietly. "We're done with him!"

"I thought he left."

"Mr. Grimmet is going to see if he wants to work at Triple Smith. They need someone to write a history of the company. He says Mr. Locke will be perfect. They'd pay him more than a teacher gets, so I'm sure he'll do it."

"Oh," Gail said. "Oh." She looked as if she didn't quite know what to do next.

"I've got to get outside!" Bonnie started down the

steps, then called back over her shoulder, "Gail? If you want, wait and walk home with us."

By the back door, Bonnie found Mr. Lipchik pretending to sweep. "Are you pleased?" he asked.

"Of course! But it was so scary winning by only one vote! And you did it. I saw you put in a ballot."

"Ah. Was that the vote you won by? Mine?"

"Yours!" she said.

"And Schaffer's, and the kindergarten Grimmet's, and Jane's and Gail's and Mrs. Tilley's, and at least two other teachers', and Miss Boyard's. . . ." He smiled. "I'd say Miss Boyard certainly cast the deciding vote for you. So did your mother and your father."

"Hey!" Bonnie said, her old suspicions about magic and Mr. Lipchik coming back. "Those were secret ballots. How do you know?"

"I watched to see who had a gleam in his eye," he said. "The second-grade Grimmet, too. Every Grimmet child voted for you but one. Lots of the fifth grade voted for you. Almost every third grader. Some parents. Jane's parents. . . ."

"Did they?" Bonnie felt prouder of that than almost anything.

"And there were two first graders, I heard them talking, who voted for you because what's-his-name, that astronaut, called you by name. Not that knowing an astronaut will be any use when it rains for a week and there's indoor recess and your kids are running wild."

My kids? Bonnie though. *My* kids? Well, only for a few weeks, she reminded herself.

"But your own was the winning vote. You can blame yourself, not me, please, when you're sitting in the office tomorrow morning and realize the stew you're in. I don't believe that 'happily ever after' stuff. History teaches: There's always the next morning."

Mr. Lipchik picked up a discarded campaign leaflet. He nodded and then shook his head sadly as he read. He tucked the paper in the bib pocket of his coveralls. "Checklist," he said, so seriously that Bonnie was reminded of all she had to do. "I'll come by the office tomorrow. We can start working on the parts for those swings."

"Yes." Bonnie folded her speech notes together with a campaign leaflet and put them safely in her own pocket and smiled again. "Yes, we can!"

"She was right on that one. Downtown's the problem on those swing parts. Downtown's a whole new story. I'd say your education in politics is just begun. Myself, I plan to get back to my studying. I've learned more about this school than I ever wanted to know, learned more names of living people. . . ."

He started to go, then turned to look at her thoughtfully. "May I give you one piece of advice, before I retire?"

"Sure."

"Tomorrow morning, you head straight for the teachers' lounge."

Bonnie winced.

"That's just what I mean. You go right in. You may have a hard time convincing yourself you're principal, and until you believe it, no one else will. Go in as if you belong there. Make yourself some tea—I wouldn't drink the coffee they have there, but the tea won't harm you and the cup will give you something to hang on to. When they see you in amongst them, they'll know who's principal."

"Thank you." Bonnie shook Mr. Lipchik's hand. "Thank you very much."

"Evening," he said, and started down the basement steps, already relighting his cigar.

Outside in the cool night, Bonnie found that the children's screaming and running around had turned into a glorious all-school game of tag, ranging over the playground, the blacktop, and the grassy field. The members of the Steering Committee had all started as It, and the little children shrieked with glee and scampered wildly away. A full moon gave plenty of light, and every dark shadow was a base.

Jumping onto a free space on the tire swing, Bonnie found Jane beside her. "Bonnie, this is so purely fantastic!" Jane said. They laughed and hugged each other and fell off onto the sand.

"And I did it without promising you a boy/girl party!" Bonnie said.

"Oh, the party's all set." Jane giggled. "I called Mrs. Dewksbury. She understood the whole problem. We're having it at her house, next Friday. Night!"

"Does Gail . . . ?"

"Gail doesn't have to come if she doesn't want to."

"Jane!" But in truth Bonnie was very pleased that there would be a party.

Five minutes later, she saw Bobby Roberts walking rapidly toward her, shouting her name. He held out his large hand and shook her small one. "Congratulations!"

"Thank you," Bonnie managed to say, although she was sure he was holding her hand longer than was necessary for mere congratulations. The newly elected interim principal of Daniel Webster Elementary School was feeling not just good, but great. She smiled modestly. "But all of you . . ."

"Okay," Bobby Roberts said. "You're It."